Paupers'

PAUPERS' GRAVES

Written by
JAMES EVERINGTON

Hersham Horror Books

James Everington

HERSHAM HORROR BOOKS
Logo by Daniel S Boucher

Cover Design by Neil Williams 2016
Copyright 2016 © Hersham Horror Books
Story copyright James Everington 2016
ISBN: 978-1533549310

All rights belong to the original artists, and writers for their contributed works.

All rights reserved. No part of this book may be reproduced, scanned or distributed in any form, including digital and electronic or mechanical, including photocopying, recording, or by any information storage and retrieval system, without the prior written consent of the Publisher, except for brief quotes for use in reviews.

This book is a work of fiction. Characters, names, places and incidents either are the product of the author's imagination or are used fictitiously, and any resemblance to any actual persons, living or dead, events, or locales is entirely coincidental.

The Primal Range
First Edition.
First published in 2016

Paupers' Graves

Also from
Hersham Horror Books:

Alt-Series

Alt-Dead
Alt-Zombie

PentAnth-Series

Fogbound From 5
Siblings
Anatomy of Death
Demons & Devilry
Dead Water

The Cursed Series

The Curse of the Mummy
The Curse of the Wolf
The Curse of the Ghost
The Curse of the Zombie
The Curse of the Monster
The Curse of the Vampire

Author's note: this story is set in the Nottingham I see when I close my eyes, not the one I see when I look out my window.
There may be differences.

PAUPERS' GRAVES

The gates to the cemetery were unlocked again; they swung open at her approach as if in welcome.

Katherine hoped it was because the others were there before her, but it was more likely Murphy had forgotten to lock up the previous night. Which meant yet again they'd be lager cans, cigarette butts, and who knew what scattered inside. Katherine pulled out a tissue from her pocket and wiped her fingers as if they were dirty. She would order Murphy to pick it up; after all, it wasn't her job to touch the litter left by the city's homeless and drunkards, was it?

She peered through the bars of the iron gate but couldn't see anyone among the tall white tombs and slate grey stones.

The Anglican cemetery sat at the intersection of two roads which carried traffic to the offices and redevelopments of Nottingham's centre in one direction and the High School in another. Roughly triangular, the cemetery's longest edge was faced by old redbrick factory buildings, converted into flats for young office workers and students. The other side was bordered by the recreation ground used for the annual Goose Fair, and opposite the main gate was Mansfield Road and a silent and boarded up church, blind to the prostitutes spilling out from the red light district further up the hill.

Katherine entered the cemetery and the gate moved shut behind her. Even just walking a few feet inside made the noise of the city's clogged and irritable rush hour seem muted. She started down one of the wide paths that wove between the outcrops of sandstone and which gave the graveyard it's distinctively undulating, flowing feel. This top part of the cemetery was spacious and tidy, the graves and obelisks arranged just so, with only a few stones succumbing to subsidence. The predominate colours of white marble and grey Portland stone were soothing to the eye, as were the smooth and beatific expressions of the stone angels eyeing heaven or bent in frozen prayer. Although they were over a hundred years old most of the graves and tombs here were free from moss and some had flowers freshly laid. Those buried beneath were from families whose name lived on; they were men who'd held keys to the city, who had been factory owners or clergymen or university benefactors (or their wives). Katherine knew their stories through study and research; she felt a certain kinship with them, a sense of shared respectability and civic pride.

But this was not the part of the cemetery which the Council wanted her to work in.

Katherine headed further inside, sticking to the curved, terraced paths although she knew the others sometimes cut corners, nervously giggling as they stepped over the graves of someone unfortunate enough to have been buried in a corner plot. She passed under a natural stone arch, hurrying slightly as she heard the derisive caws of crows from the misshapen limbs of old trees. Away from the main gate and the eyes of the street, she saw what she'd expected: a cracked super-strength lager can, a discarded and apparently unfulfilled condom, a tattered blanket so filthy it looked like it had pulled itself from the earth below. In the corner of her vision the wind made it seem to crawl to the plot of a family who had built one of the lace mills the city had once been famed for; it reached up as if to pull the stone down. Goddamn Murphy! she thought, annoyed into blasphemy.

A shadow seemed to dart between two of the ornate graves, and Katherine froze. She was somewhat near sighted and couldn't see exactly who it was who slunk away, jerking from stone to stone so as to avoid her sight. Some tramp or lowlife no doubt; she felt a moment's fright that the person might come towards her, might want something from her. She remembered her mother's breathless admonishment: *Don't talk to those kinds of people, Katherine!* Her agitation could still agitate Katherine after all these years. But the figure obviously just wanted to escape unseen (although the top part of the cemetery was open to the public during the day); maybe they though the lanyard and Council ID around Katherine's neck made her a figure of authority.

"Good riddance!" she shouted, hoping the person was still in earshot. The crows flew away at her voice, but grudgingly so, one landing nearby to eye her from a grey, crap-splattered gravestone. She saw it only had one leg, and felt its gaze on her back as she walked on.

The path narrowed and curved sharply, as if to hide what was to come from the stone sight of the angels. Two walls lined her route as it descended towards another gate, less grand than the one before. This one was always kept locked at night and sometimes during the day too. As if even Murphy understood what was beyond was shameful. She took a newly cut key from her handbag; grime dirtied her hands as she lifted the padlock.

On the other side of the gate were the old paupers' graves.

A voice called out behind her, and she dropped the key into the dead leaves that lined the path, not swept up or fully rotted since the autumn. She glared round before picking it up: the two figures behind were blurred in her vision so as to look like one.

"Saw Old Harry on the way in here," Alex said cheerfully, his voice loud in the quiet cemetery air. Katya was whispering something in his ear. "Poor bugger," he continued. "Gave him money for a cup of tea."

"He'll not spend it on tea," Katherine said in her mother's voice, and pushed the gate to the paupers' graves open.

"Saw Old Harry on the way in here," Alex said, the wind snatching at his words and making him speak louder. The smell of dead leaves hung in the air.

"Don't," Katya said into his ear, half-serious. He didn't know why she was so deferential to their boss. After all, they weren't getting paid; Katherine had only hired them as interns. But Kat did bar work and whatever else she could in the evenings to make ends meet, whereas he was still being supported by his family.

But what did money matter when you were in love? Probably in love, Alex reflected. He had no other previous relationships to compare this one too (Katya, although younger, did). Still, her warmth had felt undeniably good against him this spring morning, a reminder of the bed they'd woken up in together. She'd pulled away when they'd spied Katherine, but was holding his hand behind their backs. He missed her warmth; down among the paupers' graves it always felt cold.

"Poor old bugger. Gave him some money for a cup of tea," he couldn't help but add. In truth, they'd not been sure the figure had been the homeless man they knew as 'Old Harry', for they'd just glimpsed someone in a coat so tatty it might have been rags, moving behind an outcrop of sandstone as if he or she didn't want to be seen. But Alex knew any sign of sympathy towards the poor, never mind charity, would irritate Katherine. She was in that respect just like his family.

"A fiver. I said keep the change…"

"Don't tell stories." Kat's softly whispered words caused Alex to touch his wallet in his pocket, as if to confirm the fictionality of what he'd said. And the thought of money made him think again of the scornful girl in a blue hoodie… He tried to pull Katya closer to him again, but she refused.

Katherine retrieved her key from where she'd dropped it among the leaves, her face familiar in its pinched distaste. It was, in miniature, the same look his parents had given him when he'd said he was changing his degree course to History and again when he'd accepted the internship. "In *Nottingham* of all places," his father had grouched, whilst transferring him more money. And it would be, he suspected, the same look they'd make if and when he introduced them to Kat…

Katherine finally unlocked the gate and Katya let go of his hand as if its opening necessitated professional distance between them. The three of them walked down the path, the rough stone walls of which hid from sight the space they were descending into until they reached the bottom.

The area was roughly circular, sunk maybe twenty feet below the main graveyard due to a natural formation in the sandstone; it had been excavated to the exposed bedrock, which supported brick Gothic arches built into the walls, which were also studded with small natural caves. The hollow was known as 'Saint Ann's Valley' and it had originally been excavated in the Nineteenth Century to provide a dramatic backdrop for the tombs of the well-to-do. But the area had proved too damp and crumbling and so it had been hastily reallocated for the burial of the city's lowliest citizens in so called 'guinea graves'. Some of the first to be interred in the hollow were those who had laboured to haul away its stone. There was a single white cross with the rest of the space taken up with grey slabs of grave markers flat on the ground, weather-beaten and covered with leaves; on those where the inscriptions could still be read there were upwards of twenty names. The city poor, bundled together in the darkness, much as they had no doubt been in life.

On some of the stones the lives of those beneath were measured not in years but minutes.

At one end near to the path a space had been marked out with tent pegs; this was where their display would eventually be. Katherine and her team had been charged with creating a memorial in Saint Ann's Valley, part of the city's 'Living History' programme.

"The Council, in its wisdom," Katherine had said when interviewing Alex, "feels tourism to our city is best encouraged not by honouring Fothergill or Pratchett or Jessie Boot but by telling the 'social history' of normal people. As if the lives of the poor were dramatically different then to now... But in their words, they want a city-wide initiative to bring the past into the present." She'd looked Alex over. "You are aware of the so-called paupers' graves?"

He'd enthusiastically told her about his interests and specialisations; his study of the Spanish Flu epidemic, of the Pleasant Sunday Afternoon Society, of the working conditions inside the city's lace mills. Katherine had scowled so much he thought he'd blown the interview; the offer of a position, albeit unpaid, a week later had been a surprise.

"And the cemetery was the site of the city's last public execution," he'd said on his first day, wanting to impress. "Perhaps we could…"

"No," Katherine had said, with a shudder.

They'd spent the time so far trying to decipher or otherwise discover the names of all those unfortunates buried in the hollow. There were over a two hundred in the earth beneath the weather-beaten stones; probably more, assuming some had just been tossed in anonymously. The plan was to engrave the name of all of the paupers onto a permanent monument, as well as having displays telling the stories of some of their lives in more detail. One of the Council groundskeepers had been assigned to help them out with practical things and to undertake the Sisyphean task of tidying the hollow. And Murphy was being paid, Alex reflected, whereas he and Katya were doing it for 'experience'.

If he's being paid why isn't he here? he thought sourly, looking round Saint Ann's Valley, which seemed darker and drabber than up above.

Katherine had decided they would each be assigned one of paupers buried below to research–her boss, Coyne, had said the display must be 'personalised'. Make the dead live by telling *their* stories. When Katherine had stated that such stories would no doubt be squalid, brutish and short, it had apparently not been a concern. Maybe she should have pressed the issue; after all, her years of service surely meant her job was safe from the threatened cuts.

She had with her three slips of paper, each with the

name of one of the paupers on. She didn't know why she'd selected the three from the list she had, it had just felt right. She kept *Joseph Hewitt* for herself, and handed *Patricia Congden* to Katya and *Stanley Burton* to Alex. For some silly, giggling reason she couldn't comprehend the girl swapped her piece of paper with Alex's, said something into his ear. Katherine could only assume the girl hadn't expected Alex to react quite so frostily. She was repeating the name Joseph Hewitt in her head so she wouldn't forget it, and wondering how to tell Katya to swap the pieces of paper back, when a shadow seemed to fall across the paupers' graves.

Which couldn't have happened, for when she turned it wasn't a cloud across the sun but a person, standing looking down at them from the main graveyard, in the one place where the fence passed close to the edge of the cliff. A silhouette against the pale and dirty sky, with clothes whipped by the wind so that they resembled the ragged feathers of crows. Masculine, Katherine was convinced without being able to see any evidence of such a thing; likewise her conviction the figure was watching them.

"Murphy?" Alex called up, stupidly, for she could tell it wasn't the groundskeeper. But nonetheless, somehow, the figure did seem familiar…

The figure took a few steps forward, as if to observe them better, and she saw it walked unevenly, with a clumsy lurch as if one leg had to be dragged to align it with the other.

"Hello?" Are you lost?" Now it was Katya who Katherine couldn't help wish dumb, for the assurance of the figure's movements didn't suggest someone who was lost. It didn't reply or react. For herself, Katherine couldn't speak; she had the queer impression that the figure wasn't just observing them but *judging* them, against criteria not yet…

There was a sound behind which seemed to shatter her hazy thoughts. She didn't think it was just her who felt a moment's fright as the three of them turned towards the pathway. But the figure in her blurred vision revealed itself to be Murphy, hawking a gob of phlegm to the ground. Katya started to speak to him, but Katherine quickly turned to look for the figure again, still wondering at that strange sense of familiarity… but it was gone. Probably just one of the homeless scared off by Murphy's belated appearance, she thought.

"Did you see who that was up there?" Katya said to Murphy; something about the figure, it's almost smoke-smudged look in her vision, lingered and she felt uneasy.

"Eh?" Murphy said. "Someone was up there?" His eyes didn't look to the cliff top but remained on her.

"Yes, a man…" Katya said, faltering. She could barely recall the figure, like it had been a blotch she'd blinked away rather than anything real. And she was aware of Alex, pretending not to listen as they talked; for some reason he always got weird when Murphy was around. Katya liked the groundskeeper; he reminded her of one of her uncles back home. Didn't Alex know there was no reason to be jealous?

She'd already managed to rile Alex without meaning to, when she'd swapped the pieces of paper with their dead on.

"Here, you need to learn more about women, sweetie," she'd said into his ear. She'd meant it as a jokey reference to the prostitute they'd seen that morning, but he'd not taken it that way. His childish ability to take offence was maybe part of the innocence that appealed to her. But could someone with the money he had really be so innocent?

"Want me to go up and see who…?" Murphy was saying.

Before Katya could speak Katherine butted in: "It was just some *tramp*," she said. "No doubt he's been here all night because the gate was left open. So stop wasting time; this place won't tidy itself now will it?"

And Murphy did, Katya saw, without a word of protest for all his supposed rebelliousness. She turned away meaning to try to patch things up with Alex, but she saw he was already moodily walking away from her. He was looking at the slabs of the paupers' graves on the ground.

"Patricia Congden, Patricia Congden…" he said under his breath, as if repeating her name could help him find the spot she was buried in. Evidently it worked–he took out his tablet and took a picture of one of the graves, then started typing something on it.

"You're working *here?*" Katherine's voice said across Saint Ann's Valley.

"4G," he replied absently. "I can access the…"

"Fine, fine," Katherine interupted, turning to leave. The leaves Murphy had begun to rake were already moving as if against the wind into her path. "I assume the same applies to you?" she said to Katya.

How does she think *I* could afford a tablet? Katya wondered. (Alex had offered to buy her one, but she'd refused.) She was about to ask Katherine's for a lift back to the office to make her point, but she glanced over at Alex, who was still moodily avoiding her gaze.

Damn him, she thought affectionately, and told Katherine she was staying.

Katherine worked on the eight floor of a building of coloured glass and exposed steel, which overlooked the city centre. The ground floor was open to the public and had digital displays about D.H Lawrence, Byron, and Robin Hood (at least one of whom Katherine approved of). She hurried past their pixelated faces and the people gawping, past the security guard whose name she didn't know, and into a mirrored lift.

At her floor she stepped out into a deserted corridor, lined with old sepia photographs of Nottingham. She walked quickly to the room that served as both her office and an unofficial meeting room for her team. The room and its furnishings still felt new, as if just unwrapped; still smelt new, if an absence of odour could be called a smell. At the far end was a large window, the view from which was like being suspended above the city, able to admire the Fothergill architecture and Council House dome without being reminded of the sweat and gabble of the people below, pushing in and out of shopping centres, fast food restaurants, and bars. She could see the beginning of the long straight road which led back up to the cemetery, then past the new site for the Goose Fair (it had moved from the Market Square before Katherine had even been born, but she made a point to still say 'new'), past the old poorhouse (now a care home) and out of the city.

Katherine sighed. She thought about the old offices where she'd started her working life, with their aura of age and respectability, dim light falling slowly like dust from smudged windows onto worn carpets. The building was now just used to store records too old to be worth digitising, and barely anyone but Katherine and her team entered it.

Once as a child she had gone to see her father's office when he'd had to work at the weekend. It had been a tall red brick building, built in a horseshoe shape around a still cobbled courtyard used for parking. Elaborate wrought-iron gates had finished the square; as they had swung open Katherine had seen 'Est. 1856' at the top and somehow the sight had made her seem connected to that impossibly far away year. She had immediately decided her father must do something very serious and important, it having been done since 1856 (in fact the company manufactured wooden and steel-cast toys). It was an impression reinforced when they went inside, for the dimmed lights and silence had given the corridors something of the feel of a church. She knew now of course it was just because the building had been deserted at the weekend, but the memory remained with her nonetheless. When she and her mother had approached her father's office they'd heard him shouting from down the corridor. "It's because he's important," her mother had whispered, "and sometimes the people who work for Daddy are not all they could be" and Katherine had wondered if her mother meant Braithwaite who was the only of her father's co-workers she'd met and who *was* very skinny. But when they had gone into her father's office, they had found him alone. Katherine had thought he smelt like he sometimes did when he kissed her goodnight, when he sometimes talked funny.

She had never visited her father's workplace again.

Katherine forced herself away from the window, and to the present–she had work to do. On the whiteboard on one side of the room she wrote the names Stanley Burton, Patricia Congden and Joseph Hewitt, circling the latter. She started to write down a few ideas beneath his name;

she might need to do some research in the old Council records at some point, but it was hardly worth dirtying her hands now. She knew how people of that class had lived then; indeed, it wasn't very different to how they lived now. She thought of the fast food cartoons tossed over the cemetery fence, the syringes and beer bottles, the ragged blanket moving through the graveyard dirt. She just needed to dress Joseph Hewitt in the equivalent rags, gives his eyes the glaze of a dipsomaniac, stuff his belly out with hunger.

Have him walk with a limp that jerks his whole body, she thought.

Alex returned Kat's smile, not knowing if he really wanted her to stay in the graveyard with him or not. "You need to learn more about women,"–he knew she'd meant it as a joke but, coupled with the incident this morning it had left him wondering just how naive she thought he was. How naive he *actually* was, compared to her previous lovers.

They'd been walking towards the cemetery from Katya's bedsit (Alex lived on the other side of the river, so it was easier to go back to hers after a night out). They'd already been some tension between them, for Alex had asked why they didn't just call a taxi, but Katya had said she couldn't afford it. He'd not been sure why his offer to pay had made things worse.

He'd known, of course, that their route would take them through the red light district, but as they'd walked along the tree-lined streets, past old and spacious houses now converted in bedsits and flats, he'd not considered the possibility that prostitutes might ply their trade in the clear morning light. And the girl hadn't even looked like a prostitute, for she'd been dressed in faded black leggings and a pale blue hoodie. Alex had noticed she made eye contact with him as they walked towards her, and yes there had been something brazen and attractive about her stare but he'd been holding hands with Katya–it was 8am, he was holding hands with Katya as they walked past the bored and yawning motorists in the rush hour traffic and so when the girl had said "Got the time, love?" he'd–well, he'd looked at his watch (a gift from his father on his twenty-first) and answered her.

Katya had guffawed; the prostitute, as he'd belated realised her to be, scowled as if she thought he was condescending her. "Posh twat," she'd said as they walked past. Not making eye contact again, even though he'd been looking…

"God you're so innocent sweetie," Katya had said, and he'd almost wanted to turn back round, hand reaching in his pocket for the money she never let him spend on her, to prove that he wasn't.

He glanced up from his screen, wondering how much he'd blown things out of proportion. At least Murphy had gone, the lazy sod. Katya was walking carefully between the flat grey slabs of the paupers' graves, towards the only single gravestone in the hollow. It was a white cross, in the shade of one of the high rock walls, showing not just the dates of someone's life but their military service. 1916-1918. Of course, Stanley Burton wasn't actually buried underneath the cross, for he'd been chucked in the pit along with all the other destitutes. Nearly a hundred years later the war graves people had erected this misplaced stone; Alex supposed it was a decent gesture. Of course, he thought, if Katya hadn't swapped those pieces of paper it would have been me researching his life. He'd felt odd when they'd swapped the slips of paper; Patricia

Congden's name had crinkled in his hand like money and he'd had a sense, not quite of *déjà-vu*, but that he knew things about the dead woman already. Many of the women buried in the paupers' graves would have worked as prostitutes, he knew. Maybe he just had the idea on his mind; he'd felt embarrassingly horny since the girl had insulted him earlier. What kind of men, he thought, actually *paid* for a girl? In those days, he added. How much would it have cost?

Katya crouched in front of the cross, balanced on the balls of her feet. She always seemed so poised and self-contained. Alex wasn't sure whether she was unaware he was watching her, or just didn't care.

"Hey Kat," he called.

A cute frown crossed her face, but she didn't look in his direction straight away. He called again, and she looked up.

"I'm going back to the office," she said.

"Oh? But why?"

"We haven't all got fancy toys that let us work just anywhere."

"I thought..." (He'd thought maybe they could finish work early, and he could buy her lunch in one of the pubs just down from the cemetery). "You could borrow it, Kat, if you ever wanted..."

"That's very sweet of you but... Look, we're not a couple at work, okay? I need them to treat me seriously, I need them to take me on properly after this." She was speaking quickly, which made her accent more pronounced. "So I need to stand on my own two feet, okay? Especially as I think *she* knows..."

It was another bone of contention between them; he thought they should just admit to Katherine they were a couple whereas Katya, despite being the more affectionate in public, refused.

"Okay, sure Kat," he said, stung. "So you've said." He tried to stop his body language betraying him as she leant forward to kiss him on the mouth–chastely, as if the dead might report back any sign of passion. He reached to touch her hip but she'd already turned towards the path that led up to the main graveyard.

He tried to turn his concentration back on his work, typing up some ideas. *Possible prostitute?*–Katherine would love *that*, he thought. But facts were facts. What did prostitutes even look like in those days, he wondered, how had they been identifiable in such a prudish period? He would have to look into that. When he tried to imagine what Patricia Congden might have looked like, he saw blue eyes both haughty and needy at the same time.

The sky above reflected his restless mood, changing colour and churning with pent up clouds. He convinced himself it was about to rain and put his tablet away. Before leaving he checked he had his key to the graves. As the last one here he would need to lock up Saint Ann's Valley; Katherine had ordered it be closed to the public until the exhibition was ready. He looked behind him before he left.

"Murphy?" he called stupidly, because hadn't the groundskeeper left? There was nowhere to hide in the hollow: all but that one white gravestone were flat to the ground, the few trees slender and hunched. So he knew there could be no one else down there with him, but just for a second as the shifting clouds made the shadows move he thought he saw something shrink back in the dappled light and he almost called out again. But it *was* going to rain–he walked quickly up the slope and shut and locked the gate behind him.

In the darkness, he remembers.

Joseph always ends up with a little bit of the ready when the Goose Fair comes to town. No problems paying for his lodging *this* week.

The Market Square is full of people, packed tight around the stalls, the statue of Victoria, the hand-cranked gondolas and the lighthouse slide. The air is full of organ music, the cries of the stall-holders, and the complaints of caged poultry. The smell of the food, the noise, and the mizzle dampening everything all create a welcome distraction. Especially if you were out to impress your lass, like the young man Joseph is following. The man is cocky, swaggering–one too many glasses beforehand, no doubt– and only has eyes for his companion. So much the better for Joseph.

They have seen him–the girl having turned up her nose, as if she could smell him amidst the press of sweaty people and odour of animals–but the look they had given him had been one of contempt, not mistrust. They'd not spied him following them. The crowd is packed tight together, making it hard to move, but Joseph, even with his limp, is quicker than they. He can read the currents of the crowd, feel when a wave of people pushing is about to break and reverse direction…

The lad fails to win a prize at the Emmas, his balls far wide of the grotesque figures. He takes out some coins to have another attempt, but his companion lays a hand on his arm and shakes her head, unimpressed. Joseph is angry on his behalf. Stuck up wench! She's probably no better than a slavey for all her bloody airs and graces. But it means the lad is focused on her, not his surroundings; Joseph moves closer, right behind them…

The next time the tides of the crowd change he lets himself be swept away, but not before he has pilfered what the lad had in his jacket pocket. When he is a safe distance away, Joseph stops to look. A pipe, one of the ticklers people have been buying from the stalls (which he drops to the ground), and some bronze and silver coloured coins.

Joseph isn't alone; when it is Goose Fair time every pickpocket and layabout is up from Narrow Marsh to try their hand. The normal rules about not getting inside one another, unless you want a beating, do not apply tonight, dippings are so easy. The coppers will catch a number of them, but not Joseph. The crowd makes him feel dizzy and he limps through it, pushing now, daring people not to move aside. They all do, with a look of either disgust or concern, each of which angers him. If I were a rich sort, he thinks, with a silver topped cane, you'd show me some respect then despite this leg. But he won't draw attention to himself; his pockets are full of what he has pilfered and it is best just to get away.

The Goose Fair is so large it spills out into the streets surrounding the Square and Exchange, and it is awhile before he is out of the stalls and crowds. Crates of farm produce or squawking poultry spill out into the street; straw and excrement swirl in the water running back towards the square. The rain is heavier now, but for once he is flush enough to get a drink in one of the public houses. It is dark inside, and the sawdust sticks to his wet boots. He orders a glass of whisky but its burning taste does not lessen the ugly feelings in his breast. He should feel a greater sense of satisfaction than he does–he will not need to take any stick from the lodging house madam this week–but instead he feels something bitter stirring inside. Why has he so little and they so much? What he has taken from them, risked a beating or the jailhouse for, counts for little to them. The hatred in his soul is nourished by the liquor he is drinking. He doesn't wish to live like they do but wishes, fervently, to drag them down into his world, to pull them down with his filthy hands and see how they'd cope in Narrow Marsh...

He gets another drink, cursing himself for spending the money as soon as it is in his hand. But the bitter part of him is contemplating spending more; going up the Mansfield Road to where the girls on the turf are, and having a little good time behind the church again. Last time, the whore had tried to trick him, lifting her skirts but just sticking it between her thighs and thinking he wouldn't notice the dodge. When he'd beat her, it had been in anger not just that she'd tried to trick him but that she might *tell* people; tell people how much of fool he was. His body had shrivelled any chance of enjoyment after that, so he'd beat her again. She wouldn't be saying anything about him now, he thought.

His anger feels as impotent as his lust.

When he steps outside the pub it is still raining, cold and bitter. He pulls his ragged great coat around him and lurches away towards his lodgings, the warmth from the drink already evaporated. He sees again the haughty looks from the crowd as he pushes through; they shift from his jerking stride in the same way they'd step aside for a rat, or for a crow in his black rags pecking up the filth from the street. He's seen crows up at the cemetery eating each other's eggs, even pecking the eyes out of one of their own kind–like them he does what he has to do. He is as canny as he needs to be with his twisted and unreliable body. And anyone who judges him for it can go to Hell.

He has to stop, cough into a discoloured rag as the cold

assails his body. He knows he shouldn't be out in this weather; knows what he needs is a warm fire and beef tea, but what else can he do? The anger at those judging him, at those edging away from him as he coughs and coughs, seems to swell and make his vision darken...

No, no, no–Katherine came back to herself, rising from her chair, vision spinning. The bright light of her office seemed to block her vision of something darker; the faint smell of air freshener struggled to mask something underneath. She took a gulp of the cool air, as if she had been holding her breath until that moment. There was a bad taste in her mouth. Bad, but familiar...

In front of her was the notepad where she had been writing down notes on the life of Joseph Hewitt; there was more written down than she remembered writing.

She had been researching the old Narrow Marsh slums. They'd been notorious as a home for all manner of squalor and depravity, before being torn down in the Twenties. There was no actual record Joseph Hewitt had lived there of course; but if not, it would have been somewhere equally sordid. As Katherine had made notes on the cramped living conditions, the dirt, the sanitary arrangements (for want of a better term) she'd shuddered with a distaste not entirely unpleasant. And then she'd... well, hallucinated. What other word was there? *Always say what you mean in business*, her father had said.

She'd not been able to take much of it in, but what she'd seen had been the past. That much was obvious from the cobbled streets, the men in caps and ladies in full skirts, the cart tracks running through the middle of piles of manure in the road. But mostly she'd been overwhelmed by the sensations of her own body: the stink of it, the *itch* of it–fleas? She'd seen the grime on her hands like a tan, cracked yellow nails. She'd felt the throb of a boil on her neck every time her angry blood pulsed, felt the scratch of clothes so ragged they'd done little against the wind and the rain lashing down upon a Goose Fair crowd from long ago…

Ridiculous–Katherine felt angry with herself at the fake verisimilitude she was adding after the fact. She'd felt dizzy, eyestrain no doubt, and for a few brief seconds imagined life as Joseph Hewitt. It was the pressure of course, the pressure from Coyne and his idea of populism. Bring the past back to life indeed! She didn't need any hallucinations to know that was an awful idea.

She turned away from her desk and looked around her new, modern, clean office as if to reassure herself that it wasn't going to be taken from her. Cuts were coming, after all. From this height she could see the area where the Narrow Marsh slums had been, now criss-crossed with bridges for the new city trams, and overlooked by tall hotels lit up even in daylight with corporate logos. The past built over and forgotten; most people nowadays didn't even know the name Narrow Marsh, and only knew Broad Marsh because of the shopping centre on the same spot, which Katherine could see hulking to the left. Such familiar sights anchored her, even viewed from the unreal heights of her window. Had her 'hallucination' been anything other than imagination, a reaction to her research? It just showed how diligent she was, no doubt; how professional.

So thinking she turned back to her work and felt a moment's displeasure when she saw the earth-brown smudge on the page she'd been writing on. She checked her own hands but of course they were clean. And really it hadn't *actually* looked like a fingerprint, she thought, as she brushed the dry earth away.

Katya burst up out of the dream she had been smothered by in a rush of panic, the terror she had kept under control threatening to burst around her like loose earth. As she stumbled from her bed towards the window she had that strange, post-dream feeling of not knowing quite where she was, or who. Her vision of her bedsit was smeared, like reality was hazy and where she had been more sharply focused.

The mud and the earth constantly being reshaped. The screams of horse and man. The smoke like fog, within which the silhouettes of men seemed unreal.

Katya parted the curtains, somehow expecting her hands to stain them, and opened the window the few inches it would budge. The chill air was welcome, as was the sight of city lights, the blank twenty-first century radiance of chain-hotels, streetlights and billboards. The background hum of traffic even at this hour; the shrieks and yells of stag dos and hen parties lurching up the middle of the road.

Not the noise of artillery. Not the sounds of men dying.

Katya turned away and looked back at her bed; the duvet and ragged blanket (the landlord still hadn't fixed the heating) looking like something she'd fought her way up from beneath. Thank God Alex hadn't been with her tonight, who knew what he would have thought! She'd replied negatively to his eager text, despite its uncharacteristic forthrightness: she'd never known him to actually admit being horny. Maybe he was growing up; but if he was then he'd understand why she needed to work that night. She wanted to study the books she'd taken out of the university library without Alex feeling the need to give *his* opinion on the war. Everyone in this country seemed to have an opinion on it, despite it being fought a hundred years before; a joint heritage forged by school, church and nostalgic TV. Which was no doubt why Stanley Burton's grave, alone of those in Saint Ann's Valley, had been marked with a white cross into which was carved a wreath of stone poppies. But Katya didn't have that shared heritage; her country hadn't even been independent during World War One, and whilst they'd learnt about it at school the whole nation wasn't obsessed. But she couldn't admit her ignorance to Katherine or, for different reasons, Alex. She'd spent the evening reading about trench warfare, improvised gas masks, incompetent generals and executed deserters. About Christmas football matches that seemed unreal and so-called victories won at the cost of tens of thousands trampled into the mud, which didn't.

She'd read for hours; it must have been that which caused the dream.

It was already fading from her mind, as dreams did, but her body seemed to remember. As Katya got back into bed, the duvet damp from her own sweat, she felt weak as if she'd ran a mile or... well, as if she'd stumbled through clinging mud with her body hunched, running blindly forward as shells exploded and bullets zipped past. It hadn't seemed like a battle, she'd not seen the enemy, just men in the same uniform as hers blundering into barbed wire, folding under gunfire and shrapnel bursts, falling into what would be their grave so suddenly it was as if they were being dragged down.

The dream had been unnerving realistic, and full of details she wasn't sure she'd even read. But what bothered Katya most, as she fell back down into sleep, was the secondhand sense of it. As though she, or whoever she'd been whilst she dreamt, was merely recollecting what had happened. For overlaid across the sense of fear had been a thick, choking resentment at what had come *after*.

The sense of shame and confusion didn't fade until Alex's taxi crossed back over the river. He had paid for three taxi rides that day; Kat would hate such a waste, if she knew. But she wasn't here and she hadn't replied to his text. She'd mocked him for being innocent and then when he'd sent her something more… *mature* she hadn't replied. He wasn't sure whether he wanted to see her just for sex or to talk over what he thought he'd seen.

Because it *had* been her, hadn't it? The same girl.

It had been Katherine's fault he'd even gone back to the streets near the cemetery. Hadn't *she* said there wasn't much difference between how the poor lived then and now? So it had been research. His walk through the red-light district had been research; he'd never intended to *do* anything. And he hadn't. He'd just looked. Didn't tourists do that in Amsterdam, they went in groups and even couples just to look at the girls–window shopping. And he had tried to stare at the Nottingham girls as if they'd been on the other side of a pane of glass, but they'd stared back with a blank and intimidating gaze that had sent him scuttling away through the dead leaves and murky light.

So it had been a bad idea and maybe he deserved to feel somewhat unclean about it afterwards, but surely his guilt was overpriced? And the guilt and embarrassment couldn't explain what he'd seen.

He had been heading back; he had walked along the side of the cemetery fence and then down round the corner of the Goose Fair site until the road crossed the tram tracks.

Then, with a vague feeling of frustration he couldn't explain, he turned back the way he had come, crossed the road so he was walking past the flats crammed into the old factory buildings and Victorian family homes. A few of the buildings remained unconverted, stood back from the road as if averting their gaze from what the neighbourhood had become.

The prostitutes stood at the junctions between the road and the side-streets. He had his earphones in although no music was playing; he walked quickly so no one could accuse him of lingering. But the women had seen him walk past in one direction and now saw him coming back and so their voices called out to him: "Got a light for me?", "Got the time love?", "Looking for business?". Their accents a mixture of broad Nottinghamshire and Eastern European, with the former becoming more frequent as he continued heading back.

None of them had looked like the girl he had seen with Katya that morning. They were all dressed in ways both obvious and somewhat tragic: leather skirts, tatty stockings, tottering heels. Their eyes were abrasive, confident; you'd never believe these women, like Patricia Congden, could be *bought*, Alex thought. Which was horrible, obviously, but he had to admit part of him found it attractive despite not finding the women themselves so. If he'd had the guts he would have stopped and asked one of them how much–research, after all. He kept touching the cash in his pocket, to make sure it hadn't been taken.

As he walked it was as if the light shifted and the shadows changed. The church bell was tolling, a sound he'd never heard since he'd started working at the cemetery. He stopped in confusion, feeling an odd feeling of disorientation even though he knew exactly where he was. He felt hotter, itchier; the evening was more humid and the air around him more pungent. The voices calling to him were all pure Nottingham now and some of the words they used…

Without anything seeming to have changed in his vision, he realised the girl who'd embarrassed him in front of Katya was stood on the corner before him. "Posh twat"– his face flushed in memory. She was standing at the junction by a scruffy looking barbers shop, whose window was full of flyers for local bands and student nights. Something about her looked wrong in front of that window, and Alex had to blink his eyes, unsure if it was the foreground or background which was out of focus. She was wearing the same hoodie and leggings, or at least he thought she was; he blinked away the blurriness in his eyes that made her attire look like full skirts and something covering her hair. She was staring straight at him, with a look that seemed both suggestive and appraising.

Alex was surprised when he stuck his hands in his pockets and heard the clatter of loose coins rather than the crumple of notes. Some of the coins rolled into the street; when he bent to pick them up, face flaming again, they felt unfamiliar to his clumsy hands. They were covered in grime.

He could barely see the barber behind the girl now, as if shadows were falling but selectively, for her face was still clear. He was dimly aware not a single car had passed for the last few minutes and the road he had scrambled for the coins in had seemed cobbled and dirty with mud and even loose straw…

The girl seemed about to speak but then jerked as if spooked; she looked away from him and down the side-street. Alex looked too; the garage and flats he knew were there were hidden by the obscure darkness in his gaze. But he could see a figure coming up the street; he could hear its laboured breathing and occasional, old-fashioned curse as it approached. It moved with a limp that seemed to torment its whole body.

The girl's face notably hardened; with a last glance at Alex as if expecting him to finally say something she crossed the street and headed further down the road past the cemetery; she was soon lost to his vision because none of the streetlights appeared to be lit.

The limping figure shouted something garbled at the girl's disappearance; a drunken tramp, Alex thought. Old Harry? But no, there was something aggressive about the figure, some sense of radiating, all-consuming anger towards the world that scared Alex. He found himself turning to follow the girl…

A middle-aged woman in a leather skirt blocked his path, her face illuminated by the glow of the mobile she was texting on even as she asked him if he had enough money for a blow-job.

"And if not, piss off hanging around here scaring off the people who *can* afford it!" she yelled as, confused, he scuttled away, feeling exposed in the light that spilled out from the barbers shop and made him visible to the constant stream of traffic flowing past, towards the silent and locked up church.

Katherine hadn't slept well and the shower failed to revive her. She'd been unable to shake the feeling the water was muddy with something, her sight being too poor without her glasses to prove otherwise. The feeling of not being quite clean persisted like an itch as she drove to work, not helped by an unshaven man rushing to wash her windscreen when she stopped at a junction. The sight of the dirty suds crawling down the glass annoyed her so much she pressed her horn until the man–cursing her in a dirty accent–had walked away. Which just meant he'd not rinsed her windscreen; as she drove the suds dried to a grey scum in the periphery of her vision.

She reached the centre of town, drove down into the darkness of the carpark; the electric lighting flickered like guttering candles. Time was she'd had her own parking space behind the Council office, but cutbacks had long since snatched that perk from her. Most employees used public transport because of the cost of parking, but Katherine refused. She had a vivid memory of her mother's look of pinched distaste during a bus journey, shortly after they'd moved. She remembered how tightly her mother had held her hand, as if afraid to lose her. Katherine had kept her other hand deep in her pocket, so that none of the strange, smelly people on the bus could drag her away.

On the short walk from the carpark to the office three dishevelled figures in doorways asked her for money; one more than the previous day. Most people ignored them but Katherine always told them 'no' in a loud, clear voice. The final one she refused snarled something in reply she didn't catch; she heard the sounds of him getting up from his rags and cardboard to come after her. She didn't look back. From the sounds of his pursuit he struggled walking, and she easily left him behind.

The cool light of her office was another thing she could let wash over her but which didn't leave her feeling clean. She was early and the top floor was still deserted; Katherine stood wiping her hands with a tissue and looked at the city's spires and tower-blocks, smudged and dirty with the shadows the still rising sun had yet to wipe from them.

Katya arrived first for the meeting; dressed professionally but Katherine noted the faded colour of her jacket, the button dangling by a loose thread. By contrast when Alex arrived five minutes later his clothes looked brand new but as if thrown on. He hadn't shaven, and there was something hectic about his pink-rimmed eyes. Katherine wondered if he was sick; something instinctive in her reacted to his presence by wanting to pull away, as if he were unclean. But he wasn't acting sick; when he saw Katya he gave her a big grin. He sat in the chair next to her and after a second Katherine saw the girl stiffen and frown–had Alex just touched her leg under the table? Surely not–this wasn't the old days when Katherine had first started work; when she had been young and desirable because (and only because) of her youth, and the men in the office had laid their ink-stained hands on her, or just let their equally unclean gazes linger over her.

Very pointedly, Katya said good morning to Alex as if she barely knew him; he blinked rapidly like someone trying to rid their eyes of a speck of earth. He pulled out his tablet from his bag, laid it on the desk ready to take notes. Katya had only a pad and pen.

Katherine knew when it came time to pick just one of her interns to stay on (and Coyne had been very clear it would be one at most) it shouldn't be Alex. Objectively, it should be Katya. But...

"Are we starting?" Katya said, her accent making it sound more a challenge that it presumably was. Katherine used one of her father's old tricks, turning it back round and quickly asking Katya what progress she'd made; she didn't know whether to feel impressed or annoyed that

Katya's reply was equally as quick, her work to date conscientious. (That trick had never worked on Braithwaite, either.) Alex fidgeted beside her, like a child who needed the toilet.

"Make sure you play up his part in the war," Katherine said, "don't dwell on his life back in Narrow Marsh."

"I've not found out where he actually lived…" Katya started, but Katherine waved her words away.

"Just focus on the fact he was a hero," she said. "That's what people will want to know about, not the squalor or…" She gestured vaguely towards the city outside, as if the slums were still there, behind the Ice Arena and shopping centres. She was gratified to see Katya was scribbling notes as she spoke.

"So what, he lived in Narrow Marsh," Alex said suddenly, speaking quickly and as if out of breath. "Mine was a *whore*."

Katya looked at him, not so much in shock Katherine thought, but genuine surprise. Alex had pronounced the word like one he'd never said aloud before, over-emphasised.

"Well, we certainly won't be mentioning *that*," Katherine said.

"What do you mean? I thought we were meant to be telling their stories–make the dead live?"

"Not when it's… unedifying. People will believe what we tell them, we don't have to linger on all the gory details. There might be children visit, after all. Just present your…" Katherine looked to the whiteboard "Patricia Congden as an amalgamation of the lives of the women of the time, an archetype."

Alex looked to be about to speak again. Was he trying to impress Katya? Katherine wondered. The girl certainly didn't look impressed.

Just then the door to the meeting room banged open; Murphy stood in the doorway but didn't enter.

"Got told to come to a meeting," he said. "I don't do meetings."

"Well, you're seconded to this project for the duration so you'll *do* my meetings," Katherine said, feeling on firmer ground. Petty insubordination from someone like Murphy was to be expected, her father had taught her that. Whereas she didn't know what to make of Alex's outburst, from someone of *his* background. Maybe she should tell him to take some time off if he felt unwell, but she was reluctant to do so when they were already falling behind...

"Look, sit down," she said to Murphy, who was still standing in the doorway. She tried not to notice the dirt embedded in the wrinkles of his hands as he gripped the arms of the chair. "So, we were just going through what progress everyone has made, and what tasks they have for the rest of the week–that includes you."

"Tasks?" Murphy said. "Tidying up that tramp pit is the only task I've got. No one's cleaned up down there for years. I'd be doing it *now* if it weren't for…"

"*Actually*," Katherine took relish in cutting him off, "something else has been brought to my attention that you are to make your priority. Not to do with Saint Ann's Valley but some of the tombs in the upper graveyard…"

"Where the poshos are?" Murphy said. "I thought they weren't anything to do with us."

"They've been complaints," Katherine said.

"Complaints? Think most of them are beyond complaining…" He gave a quick wink to Katya, who smiled. Katherine was grateful Alex's reaction showed she wasn't the only one who found Murphy's quip distasteful.

"This isn't a joke!" Katherine slammed the table, causing all three of them to start. "These plots are owned by well respected families, many of whom live in the city, they have pride, civic pride and they still come to tend the graves. And there's been complaints. The gravestones, the monuments–they're askew. They're sinking."

"Subsidence," Murphy said. "It happens all the time in graveyards, you know that, so why all the commotion now…"

"It's more than that," Katherine said. "It's happening almost overnight." Murphy looked genuinely puzzled. "Could the tramps be getting in and…" she began.

"Nah. They're just piss… just drunks and druggies." Murphy shrugged. "They might have a slash against the stones but that's about it. I'll take a look next time I've got a free minute, okay? But some of them are probably sinking because the whole place is built on sandstone. So you're bound to get the odd grave collapse; bound to see some of the bones coming above ground too…"

"Christ," Alex muttered.

"Dunno about him," Murphy said, smiling at Katya again. "That one probably got bunged in the pit with all the other poor sods, I reckon…"

Once the meeting had finally ended, Katherine took a deep breath, closed her eyes. But the sensation was unpleasantly like being below ground; she quickly opened them again. The meeting room remained stubbornly dark; when she looked out the window the clouds overhead were like a dirty shroud being pulled over the entire city.

She thought of a granite gravestone, weather-beaten and with dirty grey lichen obscuring the carving. Cheap, because that was all they'd been able to afford. Heard the cawing of derisive crows.

A different graveyard, but she wondered if that one was aslant and sinking, too.

Escaping from the meeting room didn't make Alex feel any better, especially as Katya and Murphy were right behind him. The bright light of the office felt like something he was struggling through as he headed towards the lifts. He had to wait and Katya came and stood beside him. He saw her glance at him. The flush of embarrassment at how he'd behaved, at the *thoughts* he'd had, made his body feel even more heated.

"She's a right cow, eh?" Murphy said from behind them. "I don't do meetings," he added.

"Are you okay?" Katya said to Alex, in a tone that implied he'd better *not* be okay, otherwise she'd be furious at him.

"Coming down with something," he said, not looking at her. The warmth of his body had faded, but it had been maddening that morning when he'd woken; he wanted to scratch but knew that would be little relief from the itch of his thoughts. The maddening, itching desire he'd felt on and off since the previous night.

Like something had travelled back with him.

"It's not in my contract to do meetings," Murphy said. "I'll speak to my rep, see if I..."

"Where is this damn lift?" Alex said, reaching out to press the call button again. He just wanted to get away from the scene of his shame. Murphy was wittering on about the union, about *them* joining the union even though they were unpaid interns. Alex closed his eyes; when he opened them the electric sign showing which floor the lift was on looked like it had been smeared in grime. He certainly couldn't read it.

"Maybe you should go off work," Katya said, in a voice still midpoint between concern and anger. "If you're sick…" she trailed off, obviously not knowing what to say.

"You know who got us all sick pay?" Murphy said. "It was the unions…"

"We don't get sick pay; we don't get *paid* you stupid bastard!" Alex said. Both Murphy and Katya fell silent at his words; wanting to avoid having to explain them he added "I'll take the stairs," and turned away, wondering as he did so if it was a good idea to leave the two of them alone. As the door to the stairwell shut behind him he heard the ping of the lift arriving.

The eight flights of stairs left him feeling even more uncomfortably hot by the time he reached the ground. He'd had to pause to get his breath a few times, furiously ignoring the buzzing of his phone in his pocket. When he finally checked his messages at the bottom all three were from Katya:

Shall I wait for you? xxx
?x
Maybe hear from you later then.

He was about to reply, but in almost doing so he recalled he texts he'd sent to her the previous night; they made him blush to recall them now. And touching her thigh under the table! How could he apologise to her?

He would buy her a present, he decided. Jewellery maybe. She never let him buy anything but she couldn't turn down a *gift* could she? He had the cash after all; the notes he had withdrawn the previous night were all still in his pocket.

Murphy stood before the figure of an angel atop the tomb of one Edwin Selmont; its cherubic gaze was meant to be demurely turned away from that of the viewer but the lopsided angle of the stone made it seem more the unfocused stare of a drunk. One of the feathered wings touched the mud beneath.

The plinth of marble on which the angel stood was the colour of the earth it was trying to rise from, covered in mud and filth. Like it had been sunk beneath the ground and had only recently risen. Murphy washed it clean with cold water; underneath the mud he saw the marble was chipped and scratched. One corner looked like it was being pulled into the earth, the reason for the angel's drunken stoop.

Odd. Murphy stood, feeling his back twinge as he did so. He knew graves sunk of course, either because of air pockets in the earth after burial or because the coffins below collapsed under the weight above. But…

He looked around the upper graveyard; there were many elaborate tombs and graves, topped with statues and obelisks or just stones designed to be taller than their neighbour. He would have sworn they'd all been roughly straight until recently; was it just what Katherine had said that made him see them as askew and cock-eyed now? Scanning the rows of graves made him think of a stormy sea, the image frozen in stone. It was disorientating, as if he wasn't seeing the world true anymore. Or never had been, until now.

And why were the stones all so filthy with mud, when it hadn't rained for weeks?

Maybe Katherine had been right, stuck up as she was, and he should lock up the graveyard at night. But had the homeless really vandalised all these graves? Murphy tended to leave the gates unlocked out of a feeling of solidarity and fellow sympathy. After all, where else could they go? The homeless shelters were all shutting down due to the cuts, despite rising demand.

He walked away through the stones, his movement making their angles seem even more unnatural, as if lurching towards him. Something moved clumsily between the graves in the periphery of his vision, but he assumed it was just one of crows hopping away. He'd do what he could to fix the graves, but that might be precious little if the ground below was so full of sink holes. And he had the Devil's own job to tidy up Saint Ann's Valley before then anyway… More work for the same pay, he'd have complained if it hadn't been for Katya. She was alright, she was–one of the workers. He'd never had anything against immigrants. Katherine and the posh-boy he could take or leave, they were both bosses at heart, despite Alex not being one in reality yet.

He stopped. Whatever was moving between the stones was too big for a crow, although something about the hunched form and ragged black attire still brought the bird to mind. Some tramp trying to move away unseen, Murphy thought. Maybe guilty because they were the vandal? But people couldn't just push a stone grave and make it move; the idea was ridiculous. Murphy glanced at the tomb nearest to him–the mud must surely have bubbled from the ground somehow, for someone would have had to lie flat to the earth to smear it there otherwise. The fact that part of it looked like a palm and two bent fingers was surely just his eyes seeing things that weren't there.

"Hello?" he called out, but the figure had vanished.

When Katherine left the Council it was already dark, the street-lighting doing little but smudging the sky a dirty grey. In her memory her father had always returned home from work after the sun had set, appearing suddenly in her sleepy vision in his suit and tie. It had made him and his work seem mysterious; his "goodnight" just before she went to bed had been a treat, had held significance. Not like her mother and the nanny, both of whom she saw in the clarity of daylight; she could never think of them as mysterious.

Until it had all changed, and her father had been at home all day too, unshaven and somehow shrunken, in ordinary clothes.

The carpark was almost comically unnerving when she reached it: its strip lighting flickering erratically, causing shadows to move between the stone pillars and across the graffitied walls. But Katherine knew there could be no one else there; her footsteps echoed so loudly in the underground space there could be no possibility of anyone sneaking between the cars and pillars behind her. Still, the place did seem even more dirty and littered than it had done this morning. Or was that just an after-effect of researching life in the old slums?

A first she was confused by how dirty her car looked, until she remembered the dishevelled looking man who had flung dirty water on it that morning. She knew his type; not so far removed from Joseph Hewitt really. Never did any *real* work. The Council was crazy if they thought tourists and decent people would want to read the stories of people like *that*. Not that Katherine had any intention of writing such things for the display. The 'Joseph Hewitt' people would read about would be *her* Joseph Hewitt– poor, yes, but not impoverished; honest, fundamentally decent, just fallen on hard times. A few diligently researched details to make it plausible, a few venial sins– but someone a lot more, well, presentable than the real thing.

After all who would ever know or even care?

The grave of Charles Cuthbert (his wife a postscript beneath), once a renowned lace manufacturer, seemed to move in the night, as if below something had stirred in the deep soil. Old Harry tried to focus on the stone, not sure if the movement had been real or a consequence of the six cans of super strength lager that had led him to be sitting in the graveyard late at night, huddled in his tattered overcoat. But it was hard to tell, for *everything* was moving and lurching in Old Harry's vision, the graves topped with tall obelisks or statues swaying like trees in a wind; even when he forced his vision clear for a few seconds they still seemed aslant. It all seemed very remote to Harry, although no doubt it wouldn't be long before he was in such a place permanently. He liked the graveyard though; some idiot always left the gates open so it was easy to get inside, and the maze-like pathways among the graves and sandstone outcrops meant no one could ever see you from the road.

Someone obviously had similar ideas–Harry saw a shape move between the stones. Another who didn't want to be seen, to judge by the way they moved. Harry had once woken from a drunken slumber in this very spot to see one of the prostitutes from the corner near the church with a client. She'd been almost as knackered looking as he, but her client had been a young lad, drunk out of his mind, so Harry had kept quiet and just watched, touching himself under his coat. He thought he'd had a better time than the boy, dumb student twat, who was so pissed he'd spunked away nothing but money before he'd angrily shoved the woman from him, called her a fucking whore and stumbling away trying to do up his flies. As the prostitute had slipped the boy's wallet and phone into her bag she'd met Harry's eyes and he'd realised she'd known he'd been there all along.

Wouldn't mind seeing something similar again, Harry thought, his lust a faded ghost of his life before the booze. Whoever it was in the graveyard hadn't gone very far, and the furtive noises he could hear did suggest there was more than one person. Harry frowned as he listened; what *were* they up to?

Old Harry picked his body from the hard ground, ignoring the familiar pains the alcohol couldn't quite kill, and cautiously moved forward to see.

In the darkness, he remembers. In the darkness he has been pulled down into, his bones mingled with other bones, he remembers.

The pain in Joseph's insides doesn't let up after he has retched in the street outside the Leenside police station; the coppers had given him as good a beating as he had given Skinny. Maybe Mrs Allen would have kicked him out of the lodging house anyway; maybe not. But there'd been no call for Skinny to stick his beak in; everyone knew he was bent so why cast aspersions on Joseph? Skinny was a chimney sweep who lived in Narrow Marsh most of the time. His work took him into the houses of the well-to-do, and it was amazing how many of them were robbed after Skinny had paid them a visit… and how Skinny would be flush for a few weeks afterwards. So for Skinny to rat on him! Joseph had seen red. The lodging house madam had always cut him slack before when he couldn't pay, always believed him when he said he had some ready coming in from some work for the stores or the possibility of something at the brewery. And it had been a nice place: Bible verses on the walls and no drink in the house, but Joseph could ignore that for some stirabout in the morning and a plate of peas and mint of an evening. Now, though, he'll have to find somewhere else.

Joseph limps away, trying to find a way of holding his body that doesn't hurt. The coppers hadn't arrested him, just took what little money he had and then kicked him in the ribs a few times. He doesn't think they've broken anything, not any bones at least, but something inside feels wrong. His anger, at the police, at Skinny, at Mrs. Allen, drives him forward, although he isn't sure in his rage where he will sleep tonight. Where is left that will take him in? It was a damned good job the coppers hadn't asked, for it might have meant the workhouse if they had and he'd been unable to answer.

The twisted maze of streets beneath the cliffs that is Narrow Marsh should feel like a refuge–he has lived here all is life, he is known and feared here, he can get things done–but instead he is full of indecision. He needs to find a way to get some money; he puts his hands in his pockets in case any coins have miraculously appeared there. But instead he feels the urge to find Skinny, to give him another beating. He'd held back outside the lodging house, but still put the bastard into half-mourning. What *had* Skinny said about him? What angers him most is how stories will get around; how people will say Skinny got one over on him. He can't stand the idea of people telling tattle on him; when people say what they want about you it means they're not afraid of you. And people have always been afraid of Joseph.

He moves deeper into Narrow Marsh; children with streaks of soot on their faces run squawking from him and he is hard pressed not to think they are saying his name. There's filth and rubble in the street, with washing lines strung between the houses despite the dirty rain. Joseph's labours make him hot and his breath is weak; he longs to take off his ragged greatcoat but where could he put it? Some sod would have it as soon as his back was turned, all talk of community be damned. The rain makes the muck ooze down the bare streets; it always reeks to high Heaven here but it is only when he leaves and comes back that he notices. It is said it's the old marsh gases, still stinking even after they shifted the Lean.

He approaches his old lodging house, thinking maybe Mrs. Allen will relent, especially if Skinny is out working. Standing out front are some of the other lodgers, passing round a bottle and the latest racing papers. He knows they have seen him even though they act like they haven't.

"Any of you sods seen Skinny?" he shouts at them, the anger in him ruining any plan of getting them to put in a good word for him. They look at him now, like he is vermin come out the muck filled street.

Managing to ignore them, Joseph heads round the back, down an alley that leads to a cobbled courtyard, bordered on all sides by the eyes of the tall back-to-backs. The place is off limit to the men of the lodging house during the day, for it is where Mrs. Allen and her slavey do their washing and take a cup of tea. A crow so damp with rain it is a wonder it can fly flaps away at his approach; he sees it only has one leg. It had been picking at some vomit from the stones and he wonders if it was his, from when Skinny had caught him one in the guts last night.

Mrs. Allen is not there; unusually no one is in the courtyard, no young ones kicked out or girls desperately pulling in washing out the rain.

The courtyard darkens; Joseph turns and sees the three men who had been out the front standing in the alley behind him, their racing papers put away but one still holding the bottle of beer. They pause at something in his gaze, and despite the pain it is he who advances on them not the other way round. None of them stop him as he lurches past, and he manages to avoid coughing until he is away out of sight.

He doesn't know where he is going, just knows it hurts less when he keeps moving. He wants to lie down and close his eyes; if he could actually lie down somewhere comfortable maybe his body would stop hurting. But the pain never stops, the itching never stops, the voices in his head telling stories about him never ever stop. His anger forces him onwards, northward past the Market Square and the pubs he can't afford to drink in, onto the Mansfield Road.

It gets dark early and the deceptive warmth drains out of the winter day, leaving him shivering in the rain as he pulls his greatcoat tighter around him. It is tattered and without most of its buttons, so the elements still bite. His vision is going dark with exhaustion, but he can't just lie down in the street when there is the risk the coppers will find him and move him on… or worse, force him into a carriage up to the workhouse. Joseph keeps going until he reaches the cemetery; some of the older jossers he had used to lodge with had worked here, he remembers, scraping away at the rock for a load of well to do bastards. But all he cares about now is scaling the railings, so he can move out of sight and stop and sit and close his eyes…

He falls clumsily into the mud on the other side, and in full view of those passing by on foot or in a carriage spends the next few minutes coughing up blood-flecked phlegm into the wet soil. When he manages to recover, he crawls away only so far as to be out of sight of those who would tell tales of him, and leans against a marble plinth and closes his eyes, the darkness both something pulling at him and something he pulls around himself tight in his anger.

Katherine came to with a start, the shadows inside her car stretching and receding in response to a dirty orange light flicking on and off. She was parked at a drive-through fast-food restaurant, her hazards flashing. It was one on her way home, she saw, although she couldn't remember pulling in. It certainly wasn't the kind of place she would buy food from. A man in a bright and ridiculous uniform was coming out the restaurant towards her; not wanting to be seen she quickly started the car and drove away. Her hands had been gripping the steering wheel so tight they still hurt, like the memory of something worse.

Katya bolted upright in bed, heart hammering with a remembered fear… The smoke of her dreams seemed to linger in her vision and in her nostrils, and she had to rub her eyes to see clearly. For a moment the dark space around her seemed to be a dingy room with religious hangings on the walls, a bedpan on the unswept wooden floor, and a spent candle before a small, smeared window… But then it was just her bedsit again. Small, stained, familiar. Not the room Stanley Burton had lain dying with an angry shame in at all. But how could she even know what that looked like?

    They'd be no getting back to sleep, she knew. Sighing, but thankful Alex hadn't come over, she got up, wrapped herself in a blanket, and decided to do some more work.

Alex put the bracelet, which was engraved 'Kat' on the reverse, on his bedside cabinet. His skin felt flushed and his thoughts unfocused; his chest tight with the anticipation of something he couldn't articulate. As though, even if he didn't go out looking for her but remained in his room and tried to focus on his research on Patricia Congden, the girl in the hoodie and leggings would be moving towards him anyway.

Bastard, Katherine thought.

The dead body had one arm flung towards her as if in appeal; she thought of a threadbare rug over bare floorboards, of a two-bar fire black and cold. You bastard she'd thought then, as well. Said it out loud. Grown-up language learnt from voices on the other side of thin terrace walls…

"Katherine?"

It was Katya's voice. So they've arrived, Katherine thought, returning to the present. She turned to look at their shocked faces, as they saw the corpse at the far end of Saint Ann's Valley.

"Just one of those homeless people," she said. "He must have fallen. As if we weren't far enough behind as it was."

"Old Harry,"–Alex ran past her and turned the body over. She heard Katya's gasp beside her. Sentimental girl, what did she care which tramp it was? The body was sprawled beneath the drop from the cliffs at the far end of the hollow; Old Harry had managed to crawl some way before collapsing onto his front. He looked like he'd been trying to dig himself a grave before he'd even died, for his hands had evidently pulled at the turf trying to reach the earth beneath; they were still clutched tightly to the sod. His mouth dribbled soil as if he'd been trying to eat it; his nostrils were plugged with it as if he'd been forced to breathe it in.

It was all so dreadfully dirty and squalid, Katherine thought, taking a tissue from her handbag.

"Must have fallen," one of the police officers said when they eventually turned up, staring up at the cliff. "Drunk."

"But it's fenced off," Katya said; Katherine didn't know why she thought she should disagree with them.

"Well there was no other way he could have ended up in here," the policewoman said, looking with distaste around the untidy and dismal hollow. "You all said the gate was locked when you arrived."

"*This* gate, yes," Katherine said. "But the, uh, groundskeeper always forgets to lock the main gate. *That's* how they get into the cemetery to start with. The homeless. If you want to speak to him my office can give you his details…"

"Jesus," Alex muttered under her breath.

"Not really our priority," the police officer said. "We need to see if anyone can ID the poor sod, that's about it. One of the local pissheads, we'd seen him about. He climbed over the fence when drunk, then fell. What more is there to say about him?"

"But…" said Katya.

"Quite so," Katherine said, nodding as if the police were employees who'd done a good job. Two uniformed men carrying a stretcher came down the slope and into Saint Ann's Valley, one of them tossing a cigarette butt into the dead leaves as they did so. They dealt quickly if inelegantly with Old Harry, before they and the police left the hollow.

"*Now*," Katherine said, brushing her hands against each other (ever since they'd found the body she'd felt like there was loose soil or dusty fibres on her fingers and under her nails), "can we please get some work done?"

It was exactly midday.

Katherine had arranged for Murphy to make a temporary wooden structure in the place where the paupers' graves monument would eventually be, so they could get a better idea of scale. She'd divided the board into four sections, with the first three headed *Joseph Hewitt 1862-1911, Patricia Congden 1888-1919* and *Stanley Burton 1898-1920*. Before coming here she'd had each of them print out on A1 sheets of paper what they'd written so far, and she pinned these sheets of paper to the wood and stood back.

She motioned Alex and Katya to step forward to read hers as an example, although she knew what she'd written wasn't likely to have much correlation with Joseph Hewitt's real forty-nine years. The man had left little trace on the world, and what she had uncovered were hardly events she wanted to elaborate on.

Joseph Hewitt was born in the Narrow Marsh slums in central Nottingham, which were his home all his life. Like most poor men of his time he had a number of jobs: errand boy, factory worker and a brief period in service. Spells of unemployment by those unable to hold down decent situations were often punctuated by petty crime. Joseph would have lived in many of Narrow Marsh's lodging houses and despite the unsanitary conditions and unrelenting poverty of the area there was a community spirit that Hewitt always valued. In later years after injuring his leg in a factory accident Hewitt became an early advocate of the abstinence movement and an active member of the congregation of the Methodist church on Parliament Street. The foundation stone for this church was laid by one of the city's aldermen in 1874 and...

"I think maybe say too much about the church?" Katya said.

Leave a pause if someone says something they regret, Katherine remembered her father saying, to see what they say *next*. But it was Alex who broke the uncomfortable silence.

"Is *any* of this true?" he blurted, still scanning Katherine's work.

"It's true of *someone*," Katherine said, "why not him? Give him some dignity."

"But surely..."

"This isn't a democracy," Katherine said–another of her father's lines. "It's my neck on the line if this gets bad publicity, not yours."

She heard Alex mutter something about her pension under his breath; she saw Katya hide a smile. Katherine closed her eyes very deliberately for a few seconds, then reopened them and dug in her handbag for a marker pen she'd brought with her. As she picked it up she still imagined something like soil on her hands.

"Never doubt who's in charge here," she said quietly, not looking at them but at Katya's text for Stanley Burton. "I don't have to take *either* of you on after this is over, you know."

She crossed something out on Katya's piece of paper. "This is not a part of the story we wish to tell. Yes, it was a disgrace how he was treated after the war, but the details of Spanish flu are not things we wish to go into *here*." She marked a few more offending sentences. "Concentrate on his heroism during the war like I told you. Other than that it's adequate. For a first draft. You'd never guess English wasn't your first language," Katherine added, trying to soften the blow.

"I…"

"As for *this*." She turned to Alex's sheet of paper. "I told you not to mention she was a prostitute. Have you mentioned *anything* else?"

She drew two diagonal lines on the paper, crossing through the whole thing.

She wondered if she'd gone too far, but she couldn't read the look in Alex's eyes. Her criticism of his work didn't seem to have affected him as much as it should have. His eyes moved around the hollow, to Katya and away, as if something he'd anticipated might be about to happen. And Katherine couldn't help the feeling that Alex looked grubby, stained, although when she actually looked there was no visible reason for her aversion. She wondered if she had his parents' details on record, and whether she should contact them to say their son might be sick if so.

"That person's back," Katya said, cutting off her train of thought. She followed the girl's pointed finger to look up to the top of the sandstone cliffs. The same figure as a few days ago was stood in the same place, in the same oddly balanced pose. It was as black and ragged in silhouette as the crows cawing into the grey sky behind.

No one spoke this time, nor did the figure limp forward. The sheets of paper pinned to the board behind them made a noise in the breeze. How long has he been there? Katherine thought, feeling an odd unease at the notion the figure might have heard all they'd said. There was an antipathy in his observation she hadn't felt before, a hate that felt like he'd cast them down into the hollow, where the pale light that backdropped him barely reached them…

"What do you want?" Katya shouted up, with a casualness that caused Katherine to look at her in surprise. Could no one else *feel* it…? She brushed her hands against her coat. When she looked back up the figure had gone, vanished as quickly as he'd appeared, although Katherine still felt like his gaze had marked her in some way, left her coated in a filth so fine as to be invisible.

"A friend of Old Harry's?" Alex said to Katya, lightly, as if it didn't really matter. "Come to look at the spot where he…"

"Don't be stupid," Katherine said sharply, wiping her hands again.

"What a bitch," Alex said after she had gone.

Katya looked towards the path; was Katherine okay? She wondered how it would look if she hurried after to check–too much like she was trying to impress? She hadn't liked what Katherine had said about her job being on the line if the paupers' grave exhibition was a failure, because what would that mean for her own chances?

Not that Katherine was the only one acting weirdly, Katya thought, as she turned back to Alex. Ever since he'd started researching for the display he'd been acting like a horny schoolboy. Katya had been trying to get inside Stanley Burton's head, hard as that was–dying in a hovel of Spanish influenza a mere two years after surviving the war! – but Alex, she thought, was only seeing Patricia Congden from the outside; seeing the part he could buy.

"I mean, it's statistically likely she was a whore, so why…" he was saying as he stared at the pinned up paper with Katherine's X through it.

"Sweetie, whoever she was, she wasn't *just* a whore."

Alex looked taken aback, as if she'd said something that he should have known. He blinked his eyes as if to refocus on what was in front of him.

"No," he said, his voice slow like someone just woken. "No. Of course, you're right about that. I'm just angry I'm being made to gloss over the truth of it, you see…"

I wish I'd not swapped those bits of paper now, Katya thought. Alex was obsessed with whatever picture of Patricia Congden he had in his head, and she… Well, what other word than obsessed was there for the fact she was dreaming about Stanley Burton? Dreaming as if she *was* Stanley Burton. The visions of the war were memories, she knew, recalled imperfectly from his deathbed. Like he'd never been able to get over the war, like it was the only thing real to him even as he coughed his life into a dirty rag, alone in a damp and cold house in the slums. Obsessed, with the war and his bitterness upon returning. Katya had kept dreaming the same dream, pitching awake with a cry into the underground blackness of her small room ten times a night. She was exhausted now, her vision hazy she was so tired. When she'd first entered the hollow it had been like it was full of fog, or smoke, hiding from her the slabs underfoot and the far sandstone walls, creeping up and obscuring Stanley Burton's lone white cross…

"Kat? Katya?" Alex was saying; she shook herself as if free of another dream. She felt a hypocrite for thinking *him* obsessed. Had she been too harsh on him?

"I'm sorry about the… the other day," Alex said awkwardly.

"It wasn't fair on me Alex," she said, wanting to use

this opportunity to get her point across. Something about her tone of voice reminded her of Katherine; maybe part of her had been taking notes. But she did care about Alex, daft as he was. And after all, he'd been horny *for her* when he'd put his hand on her, so how could…

"I bought you something," Alex said solemnly.

She was so tired she couldn't fully hide the yawn that split her face at this; her eyes watered and blurred the paupers' graves yet again. She'd told him she didn't want him to buy her anything else, that he didn't have to express his feelings for her by spending money but she supposed if she were forgiving him it would be ungrateful of her to refuse his gesture. What had he got her *this* time? Not flowers again, maybe he'd hidden a small box of chocolates in his coat?

But the box he pulled out of his pocket was too small for chocolates.

"Alex, what have you…"

"Take it. Kat I'm sorry about the other day and you and I, you know, we…"

She took it as much to hush his garbled words as anything else. The box was so light she could imagine there was nothing in it at all; when she opened it she saw her name, shortened and engraved into metal which in the hollow's odd light looked like the marble of a tomb. She didn't want to think what it had cost, but knew it was costly enough that Alex must have used his family money again.

"Alex, I *can't…*"

"Don't say you can't take it, Kat."

"I can't take it." she said. He'd had 'Kat' engraved on it, not 'Katya'. She snapped the hinged box shut. "I can't, it would be like I owed you if I were to take it," she said.

"Kat, c'mon, do you know how much I paid…"

She had a sudden, vivid image of herself dying in the same drab, candle-lit room Stanley Burton had died in, staring at the same walls bare save for the woven religious hangings she didn't have the strength to get up and pull down. And when she closed her eyes for the final time it was like she was pulled down into darkness, pulled down by the weight of an Anglified version of her name…

When Alex touched her it was in exactly the place on her wrist where she'd imagined the weight of the bracelet. When she met Alex's gaze, there was concern there, and hurt, but also something appraising. She thrust the box back at him two-handed, as if it really were heavy. She wasn't sure what significance or permanence she meant the gesture to hold, she just knew she was exhausted and needed to be on her own to think.

"I have to go sweetie," she said and turned and ran up the slope, out of Saint Ann's Valley and into the main graveyard. In her tired vision the light looked wrong and the cemetery strange: the paths didn't seem to move through the graves and outcroppings of sandstone in the way she remembered and somehow she got lost. Tombs and stones she used as landmarks weren't present and the path itself seemed more earth than pebbled underfoot. She felt tight and angry with frustration by the time she found the exit and emerged onto the main road.

She stood trying to get her feelings back in some kind of order, let the confusion fade until there was only a dull bitterness. What am *I* angry about? she thought. She was staring dully at the green sign indicating there was a Commonwealth war grave in the cemetery. As if the Commonwealth had given a damn at the time, she thought, a receptacle for her anger rather than the cause of it.

She was about to walk away when she saw Katherine

emerge from one of the side-streets, heading back towards the cemetery. Katya turned and headed in the opposite direction before she was spotted; talking to Katherine was the last thing she needed.

But Jesus, she thought, what's wrong with her? Her boss had looked terrible; she'd been moving quickly but with none of her usual poise. Looking behind her as if being followed, Katya thought.

Alex watched Katya flee, feeling as hollow as the jewellery box in his hand did. As if there were nothing inside. He considered just tossing it away into the brown leaves, and it wasn't just thought of how much it had cost that stayed his hand. Katya had called him 'sweetie' as she'd left; so there had to be some hope, didn't there?

But it was a feeling of frustration rather than hope that returned to him as he looked around the paupers' graves. Although it was a clear day the shadows were more numerous down in the hollow and they seemed to converge towards the flat grey stone under which Patricia Congden's remains lay. Her bones no doubt scattered and mixed in with those of the others who had been buried under the same stone; they would all be intertwined, like they were fucking, Alex thought, whispering their secrets of lust and revenge into each other's ears in the dark…

He pulled his mind away from such imagery, or tried to–his thoughts always seemed both more vivid and more dream-like down in the hollow. He turned and tried to focus on the wooden frame and pinned pieces of A1 paper; 'prostitution', he read, 'tottie', 'tail'. He allowed the pictures such words conjured into his mind to linger there, while he also wondered what the point of him carrying on working for Katherine was. Did he really want the job that might be offered at the end of this internship, especially if it meant competing with Katya for it? It wasn't like it would be well paid. Maybe his parents had been right, and he should use his father's contacts to get a nice position in a bank or financial institution. He could then support Katya whilst she worked her way upwards, support she'd surely be grateful for…

He became suddenly certain someone was standing behind him, at the entrance to the hollow. He'd not heard the crunch of leaves from the sloped path, but he had been deep in thought about Katya and… other things. And who else could it be but Kat returned? He turned eagerly.

He saw the girl in the hoodie and leggings he'd seen on the corner in the red light district before. Her hood was pulled up but wisps of her blond hair were visible at either side; her eyes still held that look of both need and aloofness which he'd been picturing. He'd pictured the same look in Patricia Congden's eyes, he realised, as he'd worked: the need for his money. Pictured it in Katya's, too.

"Uh, hi," he said. "You startled me." His body felt sensitive to the itchiness of his clothes, to the dirt and sweat of him. His breath already felt tight with the effort of dousing his desire for her.

He always felt the need to keep speaking if another person didn't: "Are you here to look at the graves?" She didn't take her eyes from him. "Are you looking for anyone in particular, a relative? They're quite hard to read, but I've got all the names on my tablet, uh, I could help you…"

"Wanting business?" the girl said; her voice had such a broad north Nottingham accent it was like she'd never travelled, never had the rough edges smoothed by exposure to TV or…

"I haven't any money," Alex said truthfully (although he was aware he wasn't actually answering the question), for he'd spent all he'd withdrawn on Katya's bracelet. He put his hands in his pockets as if to pull them inside-out to demonstrate; stopped in confusion as he felt metallic coins in there, warm from his own febrile body-heat.

When he took them out he saw Queen Victoria's profile.

The girl walked over; his hand instinctively closed over the money but she laid her fingers on his and opened it up. He realised he was shaking as she touched him. She was sifting through the hot coins in his palm, seemingly surprised at how much there was. She was wearing gloves, he thought for a confused moment, when had she put on gloves?

"You can have anything you want for this," she said and he didn't resist as she took the coins from him and hid them somewhere about her person. She took his hand.

"Wait, don't..." Alex said–tried to say, for the words were just whispers caught in his throat. His thoughts couldn't progress beyond the images in his head; his whole body was itching and his vision flickered with dark patches. He imagined kissing the girl but she had a sore on her lip, and then she turned away from him, but only to brace herself against the wooden frame Murphy had built to represent the paupers' monument. He could see the words he had written behind her head. She reached back with one hand and pulled down her leggings...

... pulled up her skirts, he saw, as if reality had jump-cut. Her hair spilt either side of her bonnet and down her cotton dress. He was so close behind her she was fumbling with the belt of his jeans, and he let her. He let her hand guide him, then thrust forwards.

His head felt fuzzy as if with drink, his body felt in some way heavier, broken, but he knew despite the pain he would only last seconds. The old shame. He looked away from the nape of her neck, away from the stories he had told about her, to the flying crows like black splotches in his vision, raucous with a triumph he couldn't understand. He closed his eyes, tried to prolong the…

He thought he smelt shit and dirt and something else.

He opened his eyes just as he came; as he pulled away he realised the girl had tricked him and he'd only been fucking the gap between her thighs. He wondered, with a ferocity that seemed as foreign as his lust had seconds earlier, whether he should hit her, beat her…

When that thought faded it was like the girl had too, for Alex fell tumbling against the wooden display. One of his hands reached out and ripped a hole in one of the sheets of A1 as he fell.

He stood up, brushing the dry earth from himself… What had happened? Had he hallucinated the whole thing? As he brushed the dusty soil away it seemed to turn to mud and stick to his fingers.

His vision was clear, free of the black marks that had plagued it, and he saw the stones in the hollow were gone. The paupers' graves were open, deep raw pits going down into the muddy darkness. Besides one was a coffin, made of flimsy wood and already with a crack in one side of it. A number was scrawled on the top of it in chalk but nothing more.

Groggily, Alex turned and started to run up the slope to the main graveyard. The path was somehow free of leaves but muddy; wooden planks had been laid in parallel down it as if to aid those carrying heavy loads. There was no gate anymore.

When he was about halfway, Alex heard the sounds of someone coming up the path after him.

Katherine walked quickly away from the cemetery; she had parked her car down one of the side-roads near the High School and she wanted to leave before the chaos of picking up time. At the crossing she pressed the button and waited; there was a cheap and scruffy looking barber shop opposite, its window obscured by faded posters. A man was loitering outside smoking a cigarette; she could see through the gaps in the traffic he was looking at her with that kind of casual disdain which suggested she didn't belong. She stood straighter and tried to avoid his gaze; the wait for the lights to change seemed endless. Of course she didn't belong here, as if she would wish to! The pride some poor people took in their surroundings always annoyed her. It had annoyed her as a child, when she'd been thrust down into that dismal row of terraced houses, the other occupants of which had seemed to think they were better than her…

The lights finally changed and she crossed; the man opposite had obviously taken the opportunity to skulk back into the barbers for she could no longer see him. In fact she could no longer see the windows of the barbers at all; her vision was out of focus as if she'd removed her glasses.

Something animal, or part animal, seemed to be upon her in the middle of the road. Katherine jerked back in shock; her ankle twisted beneath her, for the road surface suddenly seemed more uneven and slick with mud. The flanks of the horses passed by, followed by the rumble of the trap they were pulling; a man surely dressed in a costume shouted something unintelligible to her as the coach went past.

She quickly scurried across, hearing as she did so the impossible sound of church bells from the other side of Mansfield Road. She looked round perplexed: people dressed as if it were over a hundred years ago moved past her, some of them briefly touching their hats as they did so. There were piles of refuse in the street that hadn't been there before, and the building that had been the barbers now looked to be some kind of general store: the windows were smaller, murkier, and on the red brick wall in large white painted letters was written: *Players Navy Cut*.

To her left, Mansfield Road itself was almost as busy and noisy as she remembered, but now with horse-drawn coaches, people in flat caps talking in the street, and the cries of a boy peddling the evening edition of papers. When anyone noticed her staring and looked back, Katherine thought they looked smudged in her vision, her short-sightedness making the soot, sores and grime on their faces more rather than less pronounced. In a daze she turned away, hurrying along the comparatively quiet road that ran opposite the graveyard rather than brave that flow of people. As she walked she glanced to her right at the taller tombs that were visible over the railings, trying to think if they looked the same.

She turned automatically down the side-street that her car should have been parked on, part of her expecting to see it, sharp-edged and *real* against the impossible backdrop of red brick factory buildings with large wooden gates and the long, familiar, charmless terraces... But her car wasn't there, no cars were there. She saw rubbish in the street and manure on the cobbled road and a rat scurrying away from her...

Katherine stopped. Closed her eyes tightly, held her breath, appalled not merely at the fact it could happen but that it should happen to *her*. She was a historian, she didn't hallucinate or make things up. (She might tidy the facts sometimes, but that was different.) This couldn't be happening…

When she opened her eyes, nothing had changed. Or rather, one thing had. The side-street was no longer deserted. A figure was navigating the piles of rubbish and coming up the street towards her.

He walked with a limp that twisted his whole body.

In the darkness, he remembers. In the darkness he has been pulled down into, his bones mingled with other bones whose voices whisper into his ear, he remembers.

Joseph thinks it best to leave The Bell before people are any the wiser; he has cadged drinks all afternoon from some lads drinking away their wages from the new railway line, as well as slipping a few coins from their pockets. Before they can suggest it is his round, he limps away.

Outside, the light is better and he looks at the coins in the palm of his hand.

Not enough to sleep anywhere other than the cemetery again.

Not that he minds, so much. There's always a few others with their head down there, but they don't bother him. It's still warm enough that he can sleep wrapped up in his greatcoat and be reasonably comfortable; if it rains (and it always seems to bloody rain) he can shelter beneath one of the arches of stone which cross the pathways.

He coughs into the street, sees a constable looking at him from the other side of the Market Square. Without stopping to look how bloody his phlegm is he hurries away, or as much as his body will let him, past the statue of Victoria and north along Queen Street. As he walks, the numbness the beers had bought him fades away, and as the pain in his body rises so too does his bitterness.

He had caught up with Skinny. He'd not beaten him, for which the lanky streak was lucky, but just asked him straight out what he had said to Mrs Allen.

"You're as much of a villain as me," Joseph had said, trying not to let the cramps inside him weaken his words. "So why were you telling stories about me being bent, eh?"

Skinny had spat into the street before replying, his face split by a grin.

"I didn't say you was bent, I said you were for the knacker's yard, mate," Skinny said. "Might be catching, whatever you've got. Mrs Allen's place is no place for someone like you, you should be in the infirmary. Or six feet under."

Now he mutters and snarls aloud as he keeps walking; if he's walking he's not bloody dying is he? How dare Skinny say things behind his back, how *dare* he? But the really scary thing is that Skinny does dare; twelve months ago he wouldn't have, Joseph knows. He pauses again in the street, his body bends double to retch against his own volition, for the pain the movement causes him makes his vision dim. The Mansfield Road is too full of busybodies; Joseph doesn't want any attention and cuts through to a road that runs parallel, lined with new terraces. The only people in sight are women and girls sweeping their doorsteps; the dust catches in Joseph's throat and he curses as he lurches past them.

He nears the cemetery, his body feeling wracked as if he had walked three times the distance. He feels a desperate urge to pee, despite knowing how painful it will prove to be. He will do it out of sight and earshot (he cries out, sometimes), against the stone of one of the bastard rich.

In front of him is a figure, stood stock still in the street as if appalled at the very sight of him.

Joseph stares at the figure, which is unclear and dim in his vision. But he can see it is a woman; she is unaccompanied but he's not sure she is on the turf. Something is odd about her, queer, but his eyes seem unable to tell him just what. His body cramps with pain as he moves towards her, making his gait the more twisted. Inexplicably, he tastes soil in his mouth and a great pressure in his head, as through the darkness he can see is something both pouring down upon him and rising up to grasp him...

"But you're... you're *dead*," the woman says at the sight of him, her voice that of the toffs who have always kept the likes of Joseph down. Which means it is unlikely she has been talking to Skinny, but what other explanation can there be for the fact she is repeating the same tales?

With a shout of anger that twists something inside of him even as it temporarily clears his vision, Joseph lurches towards the startled and improbably dressed woman in front of him.

It took Katherine a few seconds to remember that the figure dressed in ragged black *wasn't* Joseph Hewitt; that she had invented his dreadful limp, his consumptive cough. The figure that lurched towards her couldn't be a man long dead, despite what she had blurted out. Nevertheless, she could sense a malevolence from the figure, blurred as it was in her short-sighted vision.

"Stop," she shouted at him, hoping her voice didn't have the hysteria of her mother's in it. "Stop or I'll call..." But if her car was gone her mobile surely would be too.

She hadn't time to waste searching for it in her bag regardless. Instead, Katherine turned and hurried back the way she had come. The panic in her chest threatened to break free; she might escape the tramp, slow as he was, but where could she go? How could she escape the dirty and crazed world that was in the place of her own? It was nothing like what she had studied over the years, it was rawer and dirtier and *poorer* and…

At the top of the street she darted across the road and turned back towards the cemetery; that was the last place things had been normal. She thought the pursuing figure might halt at the junction, but no: instead he yelled after her, hatred in his voice like a curse.

"Liar! Liars!"

Yes, Katherine thought, this is a lie, this has all got to be a lie. A falsehood. She refused to look at the uneven street and old-fashioned shops, refused to hear the church bells or rattling carts, refused to allow the smell and taste of shit and dust in the air to register.

I reject this, I reject this utterly, she thought. She visualised herself, very distinctly, drawing a big cross through a page of old fashioned handwriting.

Before entering the cemetery, she turned to see if the ragged figure was still pursuing her; she saw he was on the other side of the road, leant against the wall of what should have been the barbers. He was coughing up something into the street; his whole body trembling with the effort and she realised how skinny he must be beneath his various rags and greatcoat. Like a crow beneath its feathers. His face was damp with sweat which ran through the grime on his face. The hand not clutching the side of the building was fumbling a rag to his coughing face, but trembling so much it couldn't reach.

When he looked up and met her gaze, this time she allowed herself to meet it. She felt her face lighten with a sneer. He was just like all the rest. For a second she forgot her surroundings completely.

She turned from him; there was a sensation like her ears popping as the noise of motorcars and a beeping pelican crossing reasserted itself. When she glanced behind her once more, she saw the barber shop back in place. There was no one outside it.

She wasn't planning to go further inside the cemetery but hurry straight back to her car, but something white was flapping on the path in front of her, making her linger just a moment. She stooped to pick it up.

It was a familiar sheet of A1 paper with a diagonal cross right through the centre of it.

Alex turned to face whoever was coming up the boarded slope behind him.

"Looking for business sweetie?" the whore said, her eyes blank as if she didn't recognise him from just a few minutes before. Like a recording reset. He found her hard to focus on; her clothes seemed to shift in his vision but maybe they were just rags whipping in the wind. She *cheated* me, he thought as she approached, thinking of the coins she had taken from his unresisting hand. But what could he do about that, despite the look in her eyes? He was spent.

He reached into his pockets as she neared, unseasonal rain falling on them both, to prove his financial impotence to her, but there were yet more old coins in his pockets. And it was like he had purchased something vital with them, for even so soon after last time his prick hardened at the sight of her, at the suggestion in her dialect-heavy murmurings.

He threw some of the coins to the ground so she had to crouch in the mud to pick them up.

Then she was on him, all sighs and entreaties for more in his ear, hands going for his pocket. He allowed her to take a few more coins, then she led him by the hand back down towards the paupers' graves.

What he saw when he reentered the hollow was like a double exposure: the open wounds of the graves dug into the earth and the flimsy coffin, but also the familiar grey slabs and lone white cross. And the same girl who was leading him by the hand was simultaneously stood a few feet away from him, reading what he had written about her on the sheets of A1 tacked to the frame representing the display. That girl was wearing a long skirt but had taken off her bonnet so her blond hair was loose to the wind; the one holding his hand wore the faded leggings and cheap Victoria Market hoodie.

The girl by the frame pulled one of the sheets of paper from it, held it above her so the wind pulled at it. With a sound of derision she let it go; Alex saw a large black cross on it as it twisted, lifted, and blew out of Saint Ann's Valley. The look of spite on her face didn't seem to fade even as she walked towards Alex; she took hold of his other arm, pressed against him so his cock strained twice as hard. Her hand snaked into his clothing and took yet more from him; he didn't mind, it was, after all, just old people's money. He was no longer sure which girl was which; either side of him they both seemed to shift and look ragged in his vision.

"You can come with both of us," one of them said, and it was only as they tightened their grips and started to pull him towards one of the open graves that he realised what she meant.

With a scream he started trying to pull free from them, but their hands were strong and their grip insistent. His feet tried to dig into the muddy ground but could find no purchase. They were still whispering into his ear as if to seduce him. They dragged him past the flimsy pauper's coffin, from which he now heard the sound of lethargic flies.

"Please!" Alex said. "What do you want? I've got money!"

At the lip of the grave they paused, allowing him to think it all a game. He looked from one girl to another– were they really the same or had he just seen them that way, because he thought he could buy them and hadn't cared beyond that? Was either of them actually the girl he'd first seen in the street with Katya? His lust for anyone but Katya now seemed not just cheap but incomprehensible. A fever passed.

The open pit of the grave was like a toothless mouth paused in the act of swallowing him whole; it had been dug deep to accommodate all the coffins and wrapped bodies to be thrown into it, Alex knew; another would hardly be noticed. He screamed imploringly at the two girls again.

"Tell stories about me, eh?" one or both of them said. "Let's see what it's really like."

They didn't push him into the grave, but both fell forward into it whilst still holding him either side. And Alex was immediately blind and suffocating, as if the grave were already filled with soil and he beneath it. He tried to kick and pull himself upwards when hands, surely belonging to more than two people, clutched him, pulled him downwards. The hands were cold but insistent; limbs brushed against him as he was dragged deeper into the darkness; voices whispered in his ear as if in welcome.

The last thing left he was sensible too was one of the hands moving over his body as if still to excite him, and pulling the box with Katya's bracelet from his pocket and away.

Katya closed her eyes and let herself be dragged under; the cost of the hot water for the bath played on her mind but she tried to let herself relax. When she lifted her head up from beneath the water the steam reminded her of the tiredness which had fogged her vision in the cemetery, which in turn reminded her of the battlefield smoke Stanley Burton had recalled on his deathbed so vividly… But she couldn't *know* that, she told herself. Her dreams, real as they'd seemed, weren't reality.

The steam soon dissipated and Katya started to shiver in the cold air (she'd been extravagant with the hot water but the heating still wasn't fixed) and that reminded her, too, of Stanley Burton's end. She didn't know why Katherine's nose wrinkled every time she mentioned poverty, like it was an infectious disease of some kind, but she was annoyed she wasn't being allowed to mention Burton's post-war life. It felt like yet a further betrayal. But what was she to do? Katherine was her boss.

She resolved to forget about it for the evening, but that just meant she thought about her fight with Alex. Had she overreacted? She became instantly defensive when reminded of her lack of money. But Alex seemed to think the more he spent on her the more it proved his worth. It was a dynamic that was always going to cause tension. Never mind the fact that she was always bone-tired and irritable from working two jobs.

Katya lifted her arm from the water, saw silver drops

ringing the area on her wrist where she'd have worn the bracelet. It would have looked *good* on her. He'd bought her a gift and actually made the effort to buy her something in a style she liked. How many boyfriends would do that? Maybe she didn't always have to be so unbending. Although he'd probably got a refund for it by now.

"Fuck it," Katya said aloud, her breath a foggy plume, and reached to her phone on the bathroom floor.

Hi Sweetie, she texted. *Want to come over with some nice wine? x* She wouldn't refuse that if he bought it for her. After a few seconds she added *Kat x* at the end. What did it matter?

Send.

But Alex didn't reply.

Working? she sent him after thirty minutes, shivering in her bathrobe. She wanted to know if he was coming over or not before she got dressed again: either pyjamas or, well, *not* pyjamas if he was. But there was still no reply. After all, he did need to work on his research. Katya knew what he'd produced so far wasn't very good. But would that matter when Alex was from a 'good family', as Katherine had told her once? Katya didn't really know what the phrase meant, it being another typically oblique piece of English middle-class code, but Katherine's tone had implied enough. A family not like Katya's, for a start. Not poor.

Might as well work too then, she thought when Alex still didn't reply. She supposed he had a right to be annoyed with her. She put on her pyjamas and a hoodie over the top, pulled the hood up over her damp hair. No need to worry about looking sexy now. Not for Stanley Burton.

She started writing, and soon was concentrating so

hard she didn't know which details were from her research and which from her dreams.

Murphy rounded the corner to Saint Ann's Valley and stopped in surprise–what on earth had happened? The earth in the hollow was exposed through rents in the turf, as if someone had been clawing at it. But the tears were six, seven inches deep–had someone really done that by hand? The flat gravestones themselves were caked with filth, as if dirty hands had roamed across them. Like it had rained in the night and turned the ground to mud; but the leaves and ground in the upper cemetery were stone dry, Murphy knew.

Looking in the other direction, he saw the mockup display of the paupers' monument had been torn down, the wood supports snapped in half, only shreds remaining of the paper that had been attached the previous day. She's gonna shit bricks when she sees this, Murphy thought.

He looked up towards the drop Old Harry had fallen from, then back to the opening to the steep path. How had anyone got in, and out, of the hollow during the night? Surely someone couldn't have climbed down the sandstone cliffs, caused such a mess, then climbed back up?

He did what he could in the time he had, clearing away the broken splinters of wood and bent tent pegs, but it wouldn't be enough to pacify Katherine. He knew from his contacts in the union she was already getting grief from her superiors about how the work was going; nice when bosses fight each other rather than us lot, Murphy thought.

He bent to clean the worst of the mud from the paupers' graves; gradually the name Joseph Hewitt came clear again. Poor sod, he thought, if I'd have been around when you were I'd probably have been chucked in this pit with you. You missed out mate, it might be shit now but at least there's the unions, at least there's the NHS and holidays now. Murphy thought of the workers and destitute buried beneath their single gray stone: united in the earth like they should have been in life. And some bastards had smeared filth all over their names, as if they weren't important, as if they'd never existed.

Murphy found himself feeling frustrated on Joseph Hewitt's behalf, for a moment so filled with anger that his vision blurred. But who should he be angry at? He couldn't think it would be the usual tramps or whores who used the cemetery who'd done this; why would they? Students, Murphy thought, some kind of student prank whilst high? Murphy had never been to university and had little time for those who had.

Maybe Katherine had been right and the damage in the upper graveyard had been caused deliberately rather than by the earth shifting; he didn't care so much about that but the vandalism of the paupers' graves was different. And not just for the fact it would cause him more work.

Murphy had other sites on his rounds that day; he walked back up the path towards the gate and locked it behind him. He'd report to his superiors what had happened in a bit; let *them* tell Katherine. She'd blame him, no doubt, but it wasn't because of that he was going to make sure it didn't happen again...

If the little twats came back that night, Murphy would be waiting for them.

Katherine hurried from the carpark, grateful to be outside of its confines. But the streets weren't any better, for it seemed dirty everywhere. There was a faint line of muck at the base of all the buildings as if a flood had risen and receded. Dead leaves black with mould or grime moved lethargically underfoot as she walked and there was actually a pile of horse excrement in the Market Square– had there been a parade or something? Did the cuts really mean there was no one to clean up dung in the street? She couldn't believe it that bad. There was no need for the Council's 'living history' initiative, Katherine thought as she stepped around scraps of paper, wet sawdust, potato peels and other unidentifiable things on the pavement. We're already living it. In Joseph Hewitt's time, she knew, rubbish had been left to pile in the streets like this; when it had decomposed enough someone came round with a cart and shovel to collect it for fertiliser. Katherine wished the damn tramps littering her way would show such initiative. How many of them *were* there? Hands reached out from bodies muffled in clothes as close to rags as made no difference. "Certainly not," she said to the requests they were too lazy to even articulate clearly. She had the feeling that yet again one of them followed behind her when she refused him, but she equally refused to look behind to check.

The Council building looked like it was being erased as she approached it, its glass architecture the same dirty grey colour as the looming sky. It seemed a poor refuge from the stink and litter of the streets but she hurried towards it, having no other.

History had once been a refuge for Katherine, somewhere to escape the vagaries of modern life. After what had happened to her father she had sworn she would never go into business. She'd spent as long as she could in academia, studying the unchanging past. That was the point–no surprises. How could there be? But then of course it *had* changed; not the past itself, not lives of the clergy and factory owners and Mayors that she wrote about, but the subject. Everyone became obsessed with making history more 'democratic', with giving voice to the marginalised, the boring, the idle. The refuge Katherine thought she'd built for herself had suddenly seemed flimsy, as if dirty hands were shaking it from outside. After not thinking about the name for many years, she'd been uncomfortably reminded of the man who'd made her feel such a thing before. Braithewaite.

Katherine pressed the button for the lift, and wiped her hands with a tissue from her handbag. On her floor the doors were slow to open as if coated in something viscous. When she stepped out and turned to put the tissue in the bin she saw it was already overflowing, a brown banana skin lolling at her like something obscene.

She was in early and there was no one else around, not even the cleaners by the look of things. How quickly the kinds of people she had to work with had made this office stained and grubby. There were black smudges like footprints on the carpets and fingerprints on the chrome rails; the very air seeming to taste of grease. She walked along the corridor towards her office, taking off her glasses and wiping them as she did so. She saw a vague shape move from the open door of her office and jerk away unsteadily. She fumbled her glasses back on–was it her imagination that saw the last instance of something hobbling around the corner and out of sight? She peeked into her office, which was empty.

"Hello?" she called up the corridor. "If you were in the middle of cleaning can you come back and finish the job? I'll wait." Her office seemed to need it; had it been occupied overnight? The carpet was littered with crumbs and dustballs, the window with the view across the city was obscured by a mark that looked like a handprint, as if someone had reached out to steady themselves, almost falling.

No one came back down the corridor.

Sighing, Katherine hung up her coat and prepared for the meeting she had called. She wiped her fingertips again, still convinced they were dirty even though she knew they weren't. It was like every surface in the office was covered in a fine, invisible layer of dirt, despite the newness of it.

Where were the others? she thought frustratedly. She'd called a meeting to get this project back on track and they weren't even…

She heard her office door open behind her.

"Do you know what time…" she said as she turned, before seeing it was her boss.

Coyne was always dressed in new suits that looking too shiny to Katherine, their pinstripes too prominent. Off the rail, she imagined, and didn't his voice confirm it? He'd gone to university but one of the 'new' ones and his accent surely showed why. She could picture the streets he came from; had in fact endured living there herself during that brief and terrible time when she and her parents had lived on the north side of the river…

Coyne was accompanied by Katya; the two of them looked like they'd been in conversation before opening the door. Although what would Coyne have to say to an intern like Katya? The girl didn't meet Katherine's eyes as she sat down.

"Is this it?" Coyne said, looking at the table with eight seats at which just Katherine and Katya were sat. "Well anyway, you can expect one less. Did no one tell you the paupers' grave site had been vandalised? Murphy is there now trying to sort it out." Was there implied *criticism* in those words, Katherine wondered. She could never tell with Coyne. He was a politician, and she didn't trust that type. Like Braithwaite.

"Who would want to vandalise those people's graves?" she said. "What would be the point?" To her mind vandalism was something done by the poor against those they were jealous of.

"That doesn't really concern us now," he said, brushing her question aside with an irritated hand gesture. He was one of those people who sometimes spat when they spoke; Katherine deplored him. "What concerns us is whether this further setback means we shouldn't pull the plug on this project."

"No," Katherine said quickly. "You can't. I..."

"No," Katya surprised her by agreeing. "We can get it back on track. We can work Saturday."

"Tomorrow?" Coyne said. "You're aware of the protest tomorrow, the march goes right past the site..."

"We'll get there early," Katherine said, before Katya could speak.

"What I *meant* was, some of your, ah, team...," Here Coyne looked around the almost empty room again, "might be protesting at the Council cuts themselves."

"I won't be," Katya said quickly, looking at Coyne. "After all, if I get the position here why would the cuts affect me?"

"And Alex?" Katherine said. The girl snorted.

"Alex? What does *Alex* have to protest about?"

"Well," Coyne said. "Well... I'll postpone a decision until next week, then. See if things are back on plan." As he went out he gave Katya an appraising look, and Katherine wondered if that would complicate things when the time came…

There was a pause; the room felt too big for just the two of them now her boss had left, and through the thin partition walls to the next room they could hear people having a loud and unexpectedly humorous meeting. The sound of voices through a wall always unnerved her…

It reminded her of *that* house, squashed in-between two others. Katherine's shock had not come from the house itself, smaller than their old one though it was, but from the realisation that if they'd slipped a few rungs down the social ladder they could conceivably slip the rest. She'd been eight years old at the time, had gone to bed every night with a tight and barely controlled panic in her chest. The sound of her father's drunken slurring and her mother attempting to keep her voice calm and precise downstairs hadn't been so bad, but the noises through her bedroom wall–the strangers' voices and coarse laughter–had made it feel like her new neighbours were right on top of her. She hadn't been able to sleep for she'd imagined them *getting through* somehow–scrambling through the attics and dropping like spiders perhaps. She lived in terror each night that she would wake up and find one of them looming over her, urging her out of bed with hands dark from motor-oil or dry earth, laughing boisterously at things she didn't understand…

She came back to the present, but her thoughts still felt sullied and greasy with what she had remembered. Was this why she felt everything so dirty and grubby all the time–because of having to work with Coyne and Murphy and Katya, whose voices and mannerisms reminded her of that hideous time? But she was being unfair.

"Thank you," she said to Katya. "For helping smooth that over. That man…" She shuddered. "Do you know where Alex is?" she added.

"No. Shall we get to work?" Katya said, as if Coyne were still watching her.

So this is how it starts, Katherine thought. I'll not miss the signs like father. Like he did with Braithwaite.

Neil Braithwaite–her father had never invited anyone from his office into their house before, but one Christmas time suddenly there he was, with his abrupt and chaotic laughter, his Scottish accent that Katherine hadn't been able to understand. He'd brought a bottle of whisky, had opened it in the lounge and gave Katherine a sniff of the bottle before her mother's horrified eyes. Katherine had wrinkled her nose in disgust, and her father had laughed a laugh that didn't belong to him.

"Neil's going to do big things at our place!" he'd said later, his voice loud and his face unexpectedly ruddy. "Shake things up; people didn't want me to bring him in but I insisted. *Insisted*, and now we're going to do good work together, eh? Shake things up?"

Already it was as though the roles were reversed, and her father was working for this loud and brash man in their home. In fact Braithwaite's rapid ascent up the company ranks had yet to begin.

He'd come around the following Christmas, Katherine remembered. Brought round another bottle of whisky as if that could make it all right. A cheaper blend. Her father had said he wouldn't take it, and that he wouldn't beg for his job back, but he'd been wrong on both counts.

That bastard, Katherine thought.

"I'm going to the cemetery," Katya said. "There's something I've forgotten to do there." Normally Katherine would have quizzed her about what it was, but today she had a reason for wanting the girl out of the office.

She waited until ten minutes after Katya had left, then opened the email she'd already begun composing to Coyne:

...*although a capable worker*, Katherine read, *the candidate does not have a broad enough range of knowledge about our County's history. She has conducted capable research into the poor of the city but the condition of poverty is generic across countries and time periods. She has little to no knowledge about the great men and women who shaped...*

Remember, you need Katya to work this weekend, Katherine thought. Could she trust Coyne not to tell?

At the thought of the name, her whole face wrinkled, as if being made to smell whisky.

Katya left the office, feeling more positive than she had done for a while. Katherine had thanked her, sort of, plus she'd met Mr Coyne as they'd both headed towards Katherine's meeting at the same time. He'd seemed to show a genuine interest in her work as she'd told him about Stanley Burton. And *he* agreed with her about how deplorably Burton had been treated. "Had a great uncle in the war," Coyne had said. "Never made it back. Almost glad, when you hear of things like this. Good work." He'd looked like he'd been about to say something else, but then they'd reached Katherine's office.

Katya walked towards the cemetery, not being able to afford to get there any other way. She passed faceless figures with their hands in pockets, smudged in her vision like the fog was something smeared across her eyes. Some of the figures at the intersections with side streets were stood motionless and posed; modern day Patricia Congdens, she thought. Maybe Alex was right, maybe their stories did deserve to be told, and Katherine had no right to order him to sugar-coat them? Poor girls out in this weather, she thought, although at least *they* were getting paid…

She was determined not to check her phone for any messages from Alex until she'd finished work.

She saw they were already making preparations for the protest march the next day: signs were up warning of traffic disruption, and metal barriers were being stacked at the side of the road. They were expecting a lot of people to march, she knew, although she'd no longer be one of them.

The cemetery was in sight but she still weakened and checked her phone before she reached it. No new messages.

Goddamn him! she thought. What right has he got not to be talking to me? Anger is the only thing she could let herself feel, for underneath was an unease, a pressure she didn't know how to relieve.

Sweetie?

She was only barely admitting it to herself, but part of the reason she'd wanted to come back to the cemetery was that she had nagging, baffling feeling Alex was still there. Which was surely ridiculous; Katya tried to rid her head of the premonition. She needed to impress Katherine–or Coyne at least–and she shouldn't let herself be distracted by worrying about Alex's vanishing act. He'd probably just gone to stay with his parents, in some big old Wi-Fi-less house somewhere in the country. There was no need to worry about him, his sort always landed on their feet. How could they not, with the money to buy anything?

Well, maybe not anything, Katya reflected as she headed towards the paupers' graves, rubbing her bare wrist.

Paupers' Graves

She went down to the hollow and saw Stanley Burton's single white cross. When she'd spoke to Coyne, she'd realised she'd never found out where Burton had *originally* been laid to rest. The cross was a recent addition, but when he'd actually been buried it must have been under one of the grey communal slabs. And Katya didn't see how they could have moved his body; the cheap coffins the poor sods had been buried in meant his remains would have mingled with the rest of them by the time the War Graves people had stepped in. She wasn't sure why she felt it important to find out, but the fact Burton had been buried in a guinea grave seemed emblematic of the way he'd been treated on his return from the front.

Katya knelt by one of the slabs, traced the faded, moss-obscured names with her fingers. Their names seemed so much less important than their dates, the short span of their years. And filled with toil and discomfort no doubt–maybe Katherine was right, maybe none of them could begin to imagine such lives and so they shouldn't be pretending they could.

But then she saw it. The names were too worn to be sure of anything, but she thought she traced with her fingers 'Stanley Burton'. One name among twenty on a slab seven feet by three. She looked at it until the letters blurred out of focus, as if she were looking through the stone and earth to where Burton lay with the others, his remains mixed with theirs just as thoroughly as if he had been killed at the front…

Katya stood up dizzily, her vision blurred and untrustworthy.

She hurried out of Saint Ann's Valley and towards the main gate. As she crossed the road to head home she saw Murphy coming towards the cemetery from one of the side-streets, although he didn't notice her. She didn't call out to him, although she knew he liked her. It might not be wise to give him any false signals. It was as much the thought of what Mr Coyne might think as Alex that stopped her.

In the darkness, he remembers. In the darkness he has been pulled down into, his bones mingled with other bones whose voices whisper into his ear so incessantly that he isn't sure if the memories are his own anymore, he remembers.

Joseph has to be helped up the steps of the church, although as soon as he reaches the top he shrugs off the guiding hands. He has come to get out of the chill; it is as cold as the grave outside, even during the day. He'd shivered all through the night in that damn cemetery and he now feels exhausted. He just wants to lie down in the comparative warmth of the church but the PSA members would never allow him that. He hates the Pleasant Sunday Afternoon Society, hates its name and sneering pretence at improving his morals. He can't read the pamphlets they press into his hands, can't concentrate on the recitals and speeches they put on. But it is somewhere to go where he can sit down, take the weight of his rag-bound and aching feet, and they can't turn him away. And at least it isn't the bloody Methodists.

He pushes his way through the men standing as they wait, still in their Sunday morning collars. Despite their mottos of brotherhood he knows they look down on him, think themselves better than him because of their jobs in the textile factories or down the pits. He can barely see them in his blurred vision; his body won't stop shivering despite coming inside and he half collapses into one of the wooden pews. One of the men comes over to him and Joseph desperately, desperately tries not to cough, because he knows if he does and the lad sees he will recoil away (at least if he has any sense) and tell the others… He snarls and flails a numb and trembling hand at the lad until he backs off, and it is only then he lets himself hack up into a rag he presses to his face.

There is the slightest pause in the men's conversation, before it begins again. Talking about me, Joseph thinks. Stories. Lies. He clenches his fist around the red speckled rag.

Anger is the only thing he can let himself feel, for underneath he knows there is nothing but terror.

At least there are no women here, he thinks as he tries to make his body stop trembling. Not allowed. The help of women irks him even more than that of men; their false kindness can harden in a second to something unyielding. Women, especially those with children, are quicker to turn away the outcast. Even if he did get hold of some money, somehow, how many lodging houses are there in the city which would take him in anymore? The last one he'd tried had kicked him out after one day, for all the other men had complained of his coughing and moans all night, and the red stains on the frayed sheet he'd slept under had proven them right. The madam had driven him off by beating him with a broom, not wanting to get too close. "Go to the poorhouse!" she'd yelled at him from the doorway, as he'd struggled to find a breath that wasn't so shallow it made his vision fade. He'd managed to mutter he'd be damned before he'd end up there, and she'd laughed and told him she believed him.

He can't catch his breath in the church either, for it is something weak and panicky inside of him. The light from the stained-glass windows flickers as if it were a guttering candle; when he looks in its direction and sees the sunlit Saints looking down on him he feels nothing but hatred. He coughs again, great wracking coughs that bend him double, seem to pitch him forward into the hazy dark. Hands are reaching for him, voices whispering to him–but those voices are liars too, with their tales of peace and solidarity in the darkness…

He jerks awake. The hands grabbing him become rough and calloused, dragging him up to his feet before he can even find his balance. The men of the Pleasant Sunday Afternoon have surrounded him and are dragging him towards the door. He snarls something in anger but also disbelief–they can't throw him out of a *church!*

"You need a doctor, mate," one of the men says. "Needs a priest," one of the others, who is behind Joseph mutters, and he tries to yell promises of violence. His struggles don't affect the ease with which they bundle him towards the church doors; the men don't even seem to understand his cries. He turns his head from side to side, trying to spit his bloody phlegm into as many of their faces as he can, but he barely even has the breath for that.

He stumbles down the steps when they let go of him, collapses into a heap on the floor. He knows he needs to raise himself, for they are threatening to go to find a copper, and then who knows where he will end up? He pulls himself upright, ignoring the blurred passers by and their noises of revulsion as they walk either side of him. He had thought the day outside was bright but it is dark now, so dark. Looking right up the Mansfield Road he sees the gates of the cemetery but he knows another night spent there will kill him. To the left the new railway station is being raised; they'd said the houses they'd pulled down were godless and disease ridden but he'd known them all his life. Narrow Marsh, still unchanged, is the other side of the city centre and he knows he'll never reach its streets before he collapses. But where can he go?

I'll be damned before the poorhouse, he thinks again.

He takes a few tentative steps one way and then the other, before he coughs so violently that he falls again. There is a ringing in his head like bells as he tumbles, and surely he falls further, deeper than the dirty street?

The hands reach for him out of the blackness his vision has become. With a final hacking breath he feels a panicked and tiny part of himself fly, leaving room for the anger and hatred inside of him to grow. There are voices in the darkness, and he doesn't know which is his own, for they all seethe.

Time becomes something at once ceaseless and unfathomable.

And then Joseph hears new voices.

Telling lies about him, and all of the dead.

Murphy had left both the gates open that night, the better to lure in the vandals. He was still convinced it would prove to be students–he'd show them, the little sods. He'd dressed in a thick coat and scarf and brought with him two blankets, a torch, and his hip-flask. The cemetery wasn't lit at night, and as he walked between the stone angels and untidy graves towards Saint Ann's Valley he was surprised how often he needed to stop and check he was on the right path. Everything looked different beneath the black sky, the dirty clouds smeared across the moon and stars. The sounds of the city, the traffic and music and sirens, had been stolen away by the night air. In reality he'd surely not moved far from them. By contrast, the sound of his breathing and the rustling of dry leaves beneath his feet seemed amplified by the night. As did the sounds of things scampering and flapping outside the beam of his torch– cats and foxes, he assumed, owls in the trees.

The hollow was even darker, a black space that his torch beam couldn't reach the end of. Murphy set forward into it, towards the cliffs at the far end where Old Harry had fallen. He directed his torch so it illuminated the ground just ahead of him, not wanting to step on the haphazardly placed paupers' graves in the dark. Those below had had their retirement disturbed enough, he thought, enraged again at the idea that people with a silver spoon in their mouth had been down into the hollow and thought it oh such a laugh to trash it all. Wasn't it enough that the rich had power over the poor whilst they lived, did they really have to exercise it against the dead as well?

He found a hole cut out into the sandstone wide enough for him to sit in, and laid one blanket on the floor and huddled himself in the other. He turned off his torch to let his night vision adapt, and took a slug of the whisky.

Now let the bastards come, he thought.

The dark sky above seemed starless and low, something which had descended to trap him in the hollow. All he could see was shadow upon shadow, and when something moved in the hollow (more damn foxes?) he had to fight the urge to flick his torch back on. He had another sip of the whisky instead, and then another. Need two or three to get used to the cheap taste, he thought, with a low-key and automatic resentment. He shifted uncomfortably, for his blanket wasn't thick enough to stop either the hardness or the coldness of the stone from making him uncomfortable. If his night vision had adjusted he couldn't tell–he couldn't see a damn thing out there in the darkness, not even the stunted trees or flat graves he knew were there.

"All that bloody Katherine's fault," he said to himself, although he knew it wasn't; he wouldn't have done this under orders or if it had just been a few of the posh graves vandalised. He didn't care about the nobs, for they had never cared about him. His life, working hard for so bloody little, had been below their radar even as he'd stared up at them in resentment. Swore he wouldn't be like them if he ever did get money or his own home.

The hip-flask was almost half-empty; Saint Ann's Valley was very still and silent, nothing moving. He would hear the disturbance of leaves or the scrap of the gate if anyone approached. Murphy felt his eyes start to close of their own accord…

And maybe he did sleep, must have done, for the next thing he knew there was the movement of people in the hollow, and the smell of freshly turned over earth.

Aha! he thought, got you, you little shits! What were they *doing*? There was the sound of people pacing around, and coughing, but no talking or nervous laughter like he'd expected.

Murphy crept forward from the small hole in the cliff, still leaving his torch switched off. The blanket over his shoulder dragged in the earth behind him, which now seemed wetter, muddier. Had it rained whilst he had dozed? But his face wasn't wet.

How many of them *were* there? He paused, for the sounds of wheezing coughs and dragging steps were all around him; there was a whole *gang* of whoever it was. Well, the posh twats probably needed the numbers to stop them being scared, he supposed.

There was a cry, guttural and caught in someone's

throat. Inarticulate but frustrated, angry even. What are these idiots high on? Murphy thought.

He stood up, pointed his torch towards the nearest noise and flicked it on.

"What do you think you're... Oh. Oh, sorry mate."

It was just one of the tramps, he saw, one of Old Harry's mates maybe, turned away and bent double beneath a blanket even more ragged than his own. Stupid sod was so drunk he didn't even turn round towards the light.

"Thought you were a kid, messing me around, see?" Murphy said. He was aware the shuffling steps all around had paused at the sound of his words. "I work here, so I was going to show them a lesson. Not that I've got any trouble with you lads," he added hastily. "I'm on your side." The figure with its back to him coughed and spat something onto the ground, next to a fresh mound of earth like someone was readying a grave.

The shuffling steps around Murphy recommenced, and seemed to be converging on the two of them.

"Want a swig of something warming?" Murphy said, fumbling for his hip-flask whilst trying to keep his torch steady. "Plenty for everyone, put some warmth on the old bones eh?" he said loudly, unnerved that none of those around him had spoken.

The figure turned, lifted its face towards the light of the torch. Murphy dropped the hip-flask in shock.

He ran, and almost made it, for they were slow.

But some of the tramp-like figures had already been blocking his route to the path up and out of the hollow; they turned towards him at his approach and he shrank from the thought of their ragged and flea-bitten embrace.

They stepped towards him, and as he stepped back

arms grabbed him from behind.

"No," he said as they pulled him downwards with a strength, an anger he could almost taste. They coughed and wheezed into his face. "No, I'm one of you! I'm on your side!"

And then Murphy was face down and tasting dead leaves and blood, his head ringing from a blow the savageness of which he could barely comprehend. And then it got darker as shapes shambled between him and the sky, and then he tasted nothing.

Katya paused as she entered the cemetery; people were already gathering at the Goose Fair site where the march would start from, and the hubbub of their voices seemed flattened by the mist. Part of her regretted not marching– after all, didn't she have as much right to complain about the cuts as anyone? When she thought about the amount of money she already owed, from student loans and overdrafts it made her feel sick inside, panicky. Her entire life was shrouded in mist, for she had no idea what lay just ahead of her... But wouldn't joining the marchers be admitting she had as little way out as them? Besides which, she'd told Katherine, and more importantly Coyne, that she'd be working today.

There was a ragged, muffled cheering sound from the other side of the cemetery wall, the beating of drums, and Katya felt guilty for it sounded like men marching to war.

Besides, maybe Alex *will* be here, she thought as she hurried inside the cemetery, hands in pockets. The nagging thought that he might be in the cemetery persisted, despite its obvious nonsense.

It must have been the mist but the cemetery seemed different as she walked through it. Did she need to get her eyes tested? For things weren't as she remembered. The impressive graves in this part of the cemetery all seemed askew or tumbled, marked with mud or other filth. There seemed to be straw and food peelings and dirty pieces of rag strewn between them, and one of the yew trees had a whole limb hanging almost off, the white wound visible. What had done that? Katya wondered. Something had agitated the crows too; they normally sat smugly in the trees but today they were all on the move, circling overhead and cawing incessantly to each other, except for one with a single leg flapping from grave to grave behind her. Was she lost? The stones around her didn't look familiar; the names carved in them not ones she recognised. The place was a bloody maze, with its outcrops of sandstone and undulating, twisting layout. And there was only one route down to the paupers' graves; if she missed it she'd have to backtrack.

She knew it would happen but the shifting fog of her vision made her see larger shapes moving between the slabs and obelisks, black, bent over and limping. Even if it wasn't just her imagination, so what, she told herself. This was a public space after all.

"Murphy?" she called out. "Katherine?" She left Alex's name unsaid, knowing if he didn't reply it would mean more than if the others didn't. Signify more to her tired mind, even if in reality it changed little.

She heard a hacking cough from someone unseen and knew it wasn't any of her colleagues. The sound seemed to move around her, as if there were more than one person shuffling just out of sight. A trick of the mist she assumed. The only figures she could actually see were the frozen stone angels, bent in lopsided prayer over aslant and stained graves.

She'd not heard the sounds of the marchers for a while, although oddly she could hear church bells. Maybe the odd weather was causing the sound to carry from somewhere else in the city. But didn't fog muffle sound?

Katya eventually found the path down to Saint Ann's Valley; on the other side of the squeaking gate there were lines in the dead leaves as though Murphy had started to rake them but given up. For all his solidarity talk he doesn't help us more than he has to, she thought.

She reached the bottom of the sloped path. It took her a few seconds to spot Katherine, for her boss was standing completely still, with her back to Katya. She seemed to be staring at something on the ground which Katya couldn't see.

"Katherine?" she called. The other woman didn't respond.

Katya moved towards her; she tripped over something in the mist and swore. She looked down; it was a boot, with dead leaves ground into its heel. It looked like one of…

"Katherine?" she said again, feeling like she was struggling to add volume to her voice in the mist. She hesitated before touching the other woman's shoulder. Katherine was slow to turn round, and when she did she looked to be somewhere else. Her mouth seemed to work at swallowing the mist in gulps as she struggled to say something to Katya.

Katya looked where Katherine had been looking; it took her a few seconds to see, for the shape was dark and laid across the slab of one of the paupers' graves.

Murphy's body looked like it had been rolled in filth and rotting leaves; his limbs were bent as if to fit his body on the slab. His face and hands were dirty with earth like he'd clawed his way out the ground. His mouth was silenced with rolled up balls of paper which had been stuffed deep inside; Katya could see it was the torn A1 sheets on which they'd told their stories of the paupers' lives.

She stood in shock, not helped by two further realisations: the slab Murphy lay on looked new and had no names carved into it, and she could smell freshly dug earth.

Something moved out of the mists of Saint Ann's Valley towards her. In the fog she thought at first it might be Alex or just Murphy, until she noticed the rags that clung to its frame, the mud and soil streaked down its face. She shrank away, but the thing was already turning away from her, moving in a rough circle around the hollow.

In the darkness all they can do is tell stories, Joseph finds. Tell stories of who they were, and in doing so imagine they were so again.

But the stories collapse, degrade, erode. He is no longer sure which parts of his tale originated with him and which he has heard from the voices of those he is interred with. And even taking the memories of others is not enough. His life and personality are gradually lost to the dark soil and he has nothing to patch and stuff the emptiness with but an old, brittle anger.

The bastard.

Katherine stared at the body star-shaped on the cheap and dusty rug laid across the bare floorboards, before the cold two-bar fire. Even in his death his newfound parsimoniousness had made him afraid to switch it on. She smelt the stink of alcohol; saw the shining glints of a broken whisky glass on the floor. That's not my father, she thought, I reject this utterly. It was very quiet, which wasn't right–her mother should have been screaming.

Why wasn't her mother screaming?

But no–she needed to keep a hold of herself. This was now; she was at the cemetery. A voice was calling her name.

She'd arrived before the others, found the gate to the paupers' graves unlocked. When she'd rounded the corner, she'd seen Murphy face down and her first thought had been he'd passed out drunk. When she'd seen he was dead her sense of time had slipped, for his pose had been a perfect recreation of her father's. But she was okay now.

But still, as she turned to look Katya, she was reminded of when she had turned to her screaming mother before someone had pulled her away, and she'd never seen her father again. Not said what she'd wanted to. If she had said it maybe the feeling that her own past had something incomplete about it wouldn't have dogged her all these years. She'd managed to classify and catalogue most of history, but not her own.

"Katya?" she said, looking over the girl's shoulder. "What are all these people doing down here? Did Murphy leave the gate open again?" For the cemetery was full of people–the *wrong* sort of people–stumbling around and threatening to mess up her project. She peered at them but even with her glasses on she couldn't make them out properly. But they were the tramps, she assumed, the protestors and the like. That explained the chunks of turf torn from the ground, the filth smeared across the gravestones. They were ignoring her and Katya, shambling with their heads downcast.

"What?" the girl said. "They aren't *people*. We need to go I think…"

"Go? We've not started yet! This whole area needs to be tidied. Can't Murphy and your boyfriend clear all these people out of here?"

Katya looked shocked; she blinked as if trying to bring something into clarity, although Katherine didn't see what she'd said was particularly opaque.

"Katherine! Murphy is dead and Alex... Alex isn't here," Katya said. "And these aren't just tramps." She waved her hand around the hollow. "We need to go!"

So it's true, Katherine thought, the girl was trying to sabotage the project after all. Should she let on she knew? Had that been the mistake her father had made with Braithewaite? Something, some memory or knowledge threatened to overwhelm her, but she closed her eyes and forcefully denied it purchase.

The people in the hollow appeared to be shambling in some kind of pattern, clockwise around her. They seemed bent under a heavy burden despite none of them wearing anything more than a tattered blanket or filthy coat. Were they searching for something? Katherine wondered, watching as they coughed and retched, scratched at themselves. Bloody imbeciles. But they were slowly drawing closer. She'd seen the crows, once, hopping almost reluctantly closer to one of their own kind, sick but still alive on the path, before they'd eagerly pecked its eyes out.

One of the tramps approached to within a few feet, his face vacant beneath an old-fashioned cap, his mouth opening to reveal grey teeth. The figure tried to speak but Katherine couldn't make out any words. Drunk already, she supposed. The man held out his hand to her; it had a dirty rag tied round the palm like a bandage.

"I'm not giving you any money. Go away!" Katherine

said, flinching back. The figure stank; they *all* stank, she thought. She felt an itch just in their presence, as if their filth were airborne, infectious. "The cemetery isn't open to the public today," she said, "go back to whatever hole you crawled from." The man didn't even make eye contact with her; his face twisted as if trying to process what she'd said and then he twisted his whole body away with a jerk.

"Katherine…"

He was looking down at the ground, Katherine saw; wringing his hands the man was looking down at the ground, moving in a spiral as he stared at the grey slabs with their list of faded names…

They all were looking at the slabs.

Her train of thought was broken by Katya pulling at her sleeve, still urging her to leave, to give up. The girl's expression was contorted but unreadable; jealous was she? Of course, they were all jealous, of what she had worked so hard to obtain. Her house, her career, her pension, her savings–she wouldn't let anyone take those things from her, wouldn't let herself be pulled down to their level…

Wouldn't be made to go back.

She pulled her arm violently away from Katya.

"I'm not leaving," she said to Katya. "And you're not getting *my* job."

She was right to confront her, Katherine saw, because the girl was so abashed at her plan being exposed she simply turned tail and ran, towards the path that led out of the hollow. One of the tramps looked up from its search of the ground as she passed, reached out for her with a new and sudden energy. Katya shrieked, flinched away in her flight and was gone round the corner. Stupid girl, Katherine thought, can't even recognise her own kind.

More and more of the people around her were looking

up, she realised, as if they had found whatever they were searching for on the flat grey gravestones strewn with soil and dead leaves.

They began moving in straight lines. Towards her.

Maybe she should run too, she wondered; she looked behind her and saw her father's body sprawled on the secondhand rug they'd had to beg someone for. She had run then, run away from home, although that wasn't how she thought of it at the time. She'd run from the tiny house with thin walls through which the neighbours' shabby lives had leaked into her own, run from the smoky odour of a two-bar fire, run from the names she'd called her father...

She blinked away tears. No, it's not him, it's *Murphy*, she thought. That drunk Murphy. Why couldn't she hold onto what she was seeing?

She turned towards the opening, to flee it all once again...

But then the first coarse, stained hand touched her, pulled her back.

She wondered if it was her father's.

Katya fled from the things shuffling in the hollow, whose bent-backed forms couldn't help but remind her of the city's homeless. She turned the corner, sprinted up the pathway towards the main cemetery.

The sound of dry leaves crunching beneath her feet faded away; she must have passed through the gate (but how could she not have noticed?) because the slope levelled off and she was into the graveyard proper–what little of it she could see in the fog that she tried to rub from her eyes, for it was so close she could imagine it something affecting her vision. She could see trees and graves in silhouette, the black arch of a sandstone formation as it curved over the pathway.

Katya turned to her right, past a grand tomb now tottering, as if pulled down by jealous hands, and skirted round the edge of the hollow. Why is there no fence, she thought, there's a fence here, I've *seen* it. But there was no sign of it, nor even of any holes in the ground indicating its removal.

She felt guilty for running and wanted to see if Katherine was okay. After all, the people (*dead* people, part of her mind insisted, dirty and stinking dead people) hadn't hurt her or even threatened her, had they? They'd just been shuffling around the paupers' graves like they were looking for something they'd dropped or misplaced…

Katya pushed through a growth of tangled undergrowth, moving carefully as she was uncertain where the drop was. She didn't want to end up like Old Harry. She cautiously approached the edge of the cliffs, and looked down into Saint Ann's Valley.

It took her a few seconds to see Katherine, who was at the centre of the hoard of the dead in their rags and tattered coats. They were all pressed right up against her so that she couldn't move; she had one arm squeezed to her side, the other straining upwards as if she were sinking. Katherine was now part of the crowd, trapped in it, and they pressed closer like she was a source of heat, the clumsy force of those on the outside causing the circle of them to turn and stagger, and Katherine with it.

Katherine had her face upturned and Katya could see she was crying, her tears leaving tracks down her pale skin, as if someone with a dirty finger had tried to wipe them away.

Katya watched indecisive, not knowing what to do. Should she go back down there and try to pull Katherine out? But the tramps (the dead...) weren't *hurting* her as far as Katya could tell; what if she made the situation worse?

She wasn't even going to give you a job, a cold part of her thought.

The dead people started pulling at Katherine, Katya saw, pawing at her. Driven by some instinct rather than trying to harm her maybe, but Katherine was now fighting to stay on her feet.

"Daddy! Daddy!" Katherine cried out, her voice high-pitched and tremulous, child-like.

She staggered; Katya saw her disappear down into the throng for a second, then she burst into view again, both arms straining upwards; Katya wasn't sure in the fog of her vision but there seemed to be fresh soil trickling from them both. And Katherine looked different, *dirtier*, her face marked and blotchy, her clothes stained and torn.

"Daddy, I'm sorry!" she cried out again, looking for all the world like she was shouting towards Murphy's body, prone on the floor and occasionally revealed as the dead moved their tramping feet from him. "Daddy I didn't mean to! I didn't mean to tell stories, I..."

And then Katherine was sucked under again, the pawing, bloodied hands pulling at her like a rip-tide. She emerged one more time and Katya had a fleeting glimpse of her now dirtied and weather-beaten face, mouth open in a shriek, teeth somehow yellowed and askew like tumbled gravestones...

And then Katherine was... gone. Not vanished exactly, but gone from Katya's sight. She could no longer distinguish Katherine from those that surrounded her.

Katya turned and ran away from the edge of the

hollow, not wanting to know if Katherine could still be heard sobbing. The cemetery was shrouded in the fog that was at once both the battlefield smoke Stanley Burton had survived and the pollution-laden mist of the paupers' past he had returned to. She wondered if that had caused the disease that killed him, and felt fouled even as she breathed it in.

There were figures moving in the mist, and she shrank from the sight because their buckled and hunched postures showed they were the same as the beings that had pulled Katherine down with them in the hollow. No, *no*, Katherine thought in a rage. Whatever was occurring, whatever had claimed Murphy and Katherine and no doubt Alex was not going to beat her. She staggered and dodged between the gravestones, trying to find a pathway she recognised. The figures in the mist largely ignored her, as if it were her now who was insubstantial and didn't match the background, not them.

Which was why she was caught unawares when one of them stepped forward with a twisted gait, and reached for her as passed. His hand grabbed her jacket; as she pulled away in fright there was a sharp pain in her ankle and she stumbled and fell.

She hastily got up, but couldn't put her full weight on her left leg anymore. She hobbled backwards; her movements paralleled that of the thing hobbling towards her. The figure stopped and stood grimly before her. He was hunched over and his body looked misshapen, bent beneath the malevolence and anger that burnt from his eyes. He was wrapped in dirty rags and blankets, further distorting his form.

"What do you want with me?" Katya said, her voice shaking. "You… you got *her*. It was her you wanted, wasn't it?"

For she knew, somehow but irrefutably, that the deformed and swaddled creature in front of her was Joseph Hewitt. Or had been, once.

"Stop," the figure said, his voice mushy. He turned his head and spat on the ground, a gesture that seemed to start in contempt but that caused a cough to wrack his body. He slammed a fist into the side of his head repeatedly, as if to force out his words even as he coughed. "Stop. Stop saying. Things. About. *Me*..." Bloody phlegm stained his lips with each angry syllable.

"Yes, that was *her*." Katya said, trying to move away and sending a bolt of new pain up her ankle as she did so. She wouldn't be able to outrun him now. She imagined him grabbing her, arms offering a filthy embrace, and all he'd have to do was hold her until the others came and they'd swarm her just like they had Katherine...

The figure–Joseph–lurched a step towards her, slamming a fist into the side of his head again. His eyes were manic and feverish; when he smiled his teeth were stained with his life's blood. His hands were half-clenched into two pinched and bird-like claws. Katya wondered how many people like him she had passed by in the street; literally stepped over in some cases.

"I'm not like her," Katya said. "I'm like you. *Poor.* I wanted to tell everyone what it was *really* like..."

More and more of the figures appeared from out of the mist from behind Joseph Hewitt, although most had yet to woken to his level of malevolence. They were all dressed in rags or the clothes of yesteryear, dirty with soot or grease or mud. Lame or toothless or with boils on their face the size of grapes. Some coughed continuously, or moaned, or scratched at themselves where the fleas bit.

Katya's words died in her throat—no idea, we had no idea, she thought. No idea about the reality of it, for all our pretty words. Crows cawed behind the hoard as if to incite them further.

"Who. Who's been. Telling stories. About. Us?" Joseph said, spitting blood. Like he was controlling them the figures were gradually straightening, flexing, as if for chase or violence. Katya backed away, wincing in pain. He thinks I'm like her, she thought somewhat hysterically, he's come back to show us how it really was... Despite the inarticulate nature of the thing hobbling towards her as if in mimicry of her broken gait it was like his words were in her head, his hate stopping Katya thinking coherently. Come back ragged and stinking and flea-bitten, she thought, and I'm just one of *them* as far as he's concerned, just like poor Murphy, just one of those who tell stories about him, and he'll drag me down to where the voices...

Despite the slowness with which most of the figures could move, they were halfway to encircling her; Katya's thoughts shrank from the idea of touching them. In front of her, to one side of Joseph Hewitt, she saw a woman whose blonde hair flapped either side of her bonnet and who was looking at her lasciviously, and on the other side a man standing erect as if to attention; his tattered and patched attire looked to have once been a uniform. "Please!" Katya said, but when Stanley Burton's gaze moved to her it was as filled with the same disgust at her lack of comprehension as Joseph Hewitt's.

As she edged further away in desperation, her hip banged against a lop-sided gravestone; the pain was sharp enough that she cried out, then quickly shut her mouth so as not to encourage the other hungry and jealous things in the mist. Were they just animated by Hewitt's hate? Katya thought, for she was thinking now, the pain having brought her back to herself. She stopped backing away, saw the haze lift from her eyes like the mist had been blown suddenly and impossibly away. All she'd had to do was force herself to see clearly. She looked at the figures, at Joseph especially, with a new clarity.

You've come back to show us what it was really like, she thought. Not the sanitised Joseph Hewitt of Katherine's lies but what you really were. But what *were* you? A disgusting, canker-ridden old tramp. So. So why am *I* afraid of *you*?

Hewitt was closing towards her, his smile an eager rictus of bloody and rotten teeth, his arms outstretched to reach for her and drag her into his world...

Katya stared at him, allowed herself to feel some of Katherine's disgust, allowed herself to hate him, hate all his wretched kind... Ignoring the pain in her ankle she stepped forward to meet him and punched him hard in the gut.

At first she thought she was wrong, that Hewitt was some spectral apparition after all, for her fist didn't seem to make contact with anything solid. But that was just because of how little of him there was underneath his layers of rags. Her blow caught Hewitt in the stomach and caused him to buckle. He's so *thin*, Katya thought distantly. He's really almost nothing.

At her blow, the other figures all froze for a second, then resumed towards her more clumsily than before. Hewitt stumbled away, clutching himself; he started coughing and would not stop. Dark, globular looking blood flecked the ground beneath him.

Her cry a mixture of fear, hate and repulsion, Katya hit Hewitt again.

Paupers' Graves

When he fell, it was if he were being pulled down into the ground, for his body was already cloaked with dirt; when he wheezed into the earth he dribbled out soil as if it were already inside of him.

Katya held out the hand she had punched him with away from herself, like it was infected with his grime. She remembered Katherine's constant wiping of her hands with tissues. Whatever moment of clarity had allowed her to see Hewitt clearly was gone, for when she turned to run from the other shambling figures it was foggy in her vision again. Part of her still wanted to turn to her tormentors and attack, to punch and kick and gouge the awful, stinking fucking scum who were trying to drag her away with them, as if she were one of them... But there were too many of them, and despite the fact she'd flooded her thoughts with the venom she'd needed to hit Hewitt, she fled instead.

Katya couldn't find the gate that led out the cemetery; the fog seemed to thicken around her as she ran, and the graves and tombs became dark and unfamiliar. She ignored the sound of church bells tolling–where the hell was home? She held her hand away from her body as she ran. Whether any of the paupers were still pursuing her she couldn't tell, and didn't look back to check.

Eventually, she heard a different noise: that of chanting and whistling. She ran towards it, and reached the metal spiked fence that separated the cemetery from the Goose Fair site. She saw people with placards and banners on the other side; if the church bells were still ringing they were drowned out by their optimistic and strident cries.

Katya tried to climb the fence, standing on one of the aslant graves in order to do so. Some of the protestors, mistaking her for one of them, came to help her down to the pavement on the other side.

"Get your stinking hands off me!" she shrieked at them.

It was three weeks later.

The leaves that littered the path down to Saint Ann's Valley had turned to a pulpy rotten mush; Katya grimaced but there was little choice but to step through the muck. She unlocked the gate and swung it open; it had been left padlocked since what Coyne referred to as 'the incident'.

Disgusting 'Protestors' Trash Graves of the Poor the local newspaper had said, also accusing them of smashing shop windows and setting alight a car in town. Katya didn't know if those bits were true. She didn't really care. After all, the protestors hadn't achieved anything had they? The cuts had been enacted, and more were to come.

The papers, and the police, and Coyne only knew part of it, of course. None of them had any idea what had happened to her former colleagues, and she hadn't mentioned what she'd seen, or thought she had: Katherine with her arms lifted for help as she was dragged down into the mass of people surrounding her.

Katya walked down into the hollow, turned to look at the mess. She hadn't been here since that day, and she half expected to see the slabs of the paupers' graves pushed aside to reveal the black pits beneath. But the stones were all in their rightful places, just stained with dirt and in some cases what looked like very old blood. The ground was churned up like the aftermath of a battle, with only scant tufts of grass remaining amidst the mud. The trees had wounds the colour of pale flesh where branches had been pulled off; the smooth sandstone cliffs had jagged marks where pieces of rock had somehow been torn away. Litter, curiously old-fashioned in nature–straw, black and white newspaper, and other things less mentionable–flapped trapped in the mud, unable to escape.

Not the only things unable to escape, Katya thought– but no. They'd found no bodies, not on the surface anyway. What she'd thought she'd seen happening couldn't have done so, nor could anything she had imagined in the darker hours since then.

She saw Stanley Burton's white gravestone had been torn down and was cracked in two. Too bad there was no money for a replacement, she thought. But then, his name was still carved on one of the flat paupers' slabs somewhere; his bones no doubt mingled beneath. Where he *belongs*, Katya thought, thinking of an unformed figure's lurching movement towards her in the fog.

Coyne had told her on day one that she only had a limited time and budget to get the cemetery looking presentable again. There would be no 'living history' display now; the new tourist information would focus on the tombs of the great and good in the upper cemetery. The paupers' graves were not going to be mentioned; they were to be kept locked up indefinitely but because the hollow could be seen from above she'd been told to make it look respectable from a distance. Katya had told him she'd need a new groundskeeper assigned to her temporarily, and to help with the literature on the upper cemetery she wanted one or two interns. Unpaid, Coyne had said, and only one gets a job at the end. Cutbacks, you know.

Nevertheless, Katya was having to constantly work late, and in the evenings felt nervous and fatigued.

Her new contract had a probation period written into it; if she was found to have underperformed in the first six months they could get rid of her with no notice or pay off. In her more paranoid moments she wondered if they would enforce that clause anyway, once the cemetery was no longer an embarrassment to the city. Katya had a new flat to pay the rent on south of the river, away from the whores and down and outs.

She had to work hard because she'd hate to go *back*.

It was silent in the cemetery apart from the crows futilely protesting her presence; she idly wondered whether the pest control department could do anything about them. She was about to turn away from the disarray in the hollow when the dirty looking clouds above shifted for a few seconds and she saw something glint among the churned up mud and trash.

She walked over and bent down, saw a link of silver chain half-buried in the earth. Her mouth a moue of distaste she pulled it up, revealing a dirt encrusted and stained bracelet that looked familiar. She turned it over, saw a version of her name (she'd started introducing herself as 'Kat' in office meetings because it was easier for her colleagues; most of them assumed it was short for Katherine).

"Kat, c'mon, do you know how *much*..." she remembered Alex saying. Do you know how much it *cost*? How much I thought you were worth?

But no it couldn't be the same one, Kat thought, turning the bracelet over in her hands. This thing was *old*. She could see that from how dull the metal's glint was, from the misshapen and bent links of the chain. It had lain underground for at least a hundred years, she guessed.

And it couldn't be real silver, could it, if it had been buried with some tramp? Dirty, grubby thing–it seemed to weight absolutely nothing in her hands, and she let it slip from her grasp back into the mud. She resisted the urge to grind it back under with her foot.

Paupers' Graves

Kat took some pictures of the destruction and mess in surrounding the paupers' graves; she would check them on her tablet later, back in her office. She wondered if it had been cleaned properly yet; she sent emails of complaint but still found what looked like splashes of grime or dirty fingerprints on the table and windows.

She left Saint Ann's Valley, not looking back, and locked the gate behind her. As she walked through the main cemetery, with its impressive and imposing graves, there was none of the mist she always associated with the site. Everything seemed clear.

Kat left the graveyard, turned towards the city centre. She crossed the road and walked past a rough, shoddy looking barbers. She was thinking what a shame it was that the historically important cemetery, with its Edwardian figure-sculpting tombs and dramatic natural sandstone formations, should be associated with the paupers and their pitiful grey slabs, when a figure barely more than rags sitting in the barber's doorway reached out a hand towards her.

"Can you… Can you help me?" it asked, a woman's voice sounding surprisingly clear and without accent. Kat barely glanced towards her.

"No, I cannot," she said firmly, thinking of her new flat as she walked away, her new rent, her clear future.

"I'm lost," the tramp said to her retreating back. "This isn't right, I'm lost and I'm, I'm *sorry* I…"

Of course it was just her mind telling stories that made her think the woman had sounded, even looked like Katherine, Kat knew. Katherine, for all her faults, had not been some down and out; in fact she was starting to realise her old boss had actually been right about many things. And besides, that woman's face had been too stretched and worn to have been Katherine's...

She took a tissue from her pocket and tried to clean her hands for even though she'd not touched anything in the cemetery they felt dirtied and itchy. They had done so a lot, recently.

Kat walked down a side street parallel to Mansfield Road towards town; she could see the shining glass of the new Council building in the distance, like a different world from the foreground of dated and scruffy terraces. And of course she didn't look back. There was nothing behind her that wasn't dead and buried. No one hunched and limping behind her, despite the stories her imagination might be telling.

She was wiping and wiping her hands, for they still felt so unclean.

Author Notes & Bio

I doubt it's much of a revelation that the initial inspiration for *Paupers' Graves* sprang from the setting: the model for the fictional graveyard in the story is Rock Cemetery here in Nottingham. Much of the detail, including the sandstone outcrops, Saint Ann's Valley, and of course the paupers' graves themselves, is taken straight from life.

It's a place that's always fascinated me and I've wanted to write a story set there for years. In fact, I did once before: a thankfully unpublished piece of crap I wrote in my early twenties. A gloomy, morose work that was about little more than the protagonist not being able to talk to girls. (Write about what you know, right?) At one point, for light relief from his own insecurities, he goes to wander around a cemetery. Because of course he does. Eventually he finds himself among the paupers' graves. I seemed to think that realisation was enough to end a scene on, that it was a dramatic enough detail in itself without it having any real connection to anything I was writing about.

God, I was a twat.

But as I say, that story never saw the light of day (if I die, burn my papers) and so I was free to use the cemetery again when Hersham Horror came calling. It seemed obvious it would make a much better setting for a horror story. But a horror story about *what?* I don't believe that horror stories are about the ghosts and ghoulies, not underneath, but about the same human things that all stories are ultimately about. At the time I happened to walk past the cemetery a few times a week on my way to the work; from the outside only the tombs of the more well-to-do can be seen; the paupers' graves are invisible. Out of sight, out of mind–much like we treat the poor today. Gradually a plot based on this similarity between the present and past, between our attitudes to the poor and the dead started to form in my mind. I knew I'd have to change some details of the cemetery to make the story work, but what seemed to me the key feature of it remained: the contrast between the grandiose tombs of the upper cemetery and the scraped-back rock and flat grey stones of the old guinea graves. A contrast that really does seem reflected in the streets outside, nevermore so than in this time of austerity.

So the cemetery became a way of writing about the wider world, a microcosm of our current divisions. But I didn't want the place to lose its reality behind all this allegory, it had to still be a cemetery. And in a horror story that could only lead to one thing: the dead coming back. But what *reason* would these dead have to return; after all, might not the poor prefer the peace of the grave after the toils they endured?

I wanted the story to in some way be true to the harsh existence that the poor of the time would have lived; and I realised that one thing that might rouse the dead back to life would be someone telling stories about them *without* that care and attention.

Because *Paupers' Graves* is not just a story of have and have nots, of austerity and the grave, but also a story about stories. The three main characters tell stories about 'their' dead; Katherine tells stories about her own past, while in their own ways Katya and Alex do so about their future. Alex projects his fantasies onto both Patricia

Congden and the modern day prostitutes he sees; Murphy tells himself stories of socialism and the comradeship of the working class. And the dead tell stories about their past lives; in fact, their stories merge into each other, much like their bodies do underneath the graves. When Joseph remembers, he remembers more than his own life; he remembers details from the lives of those he has been buried with.

The brief introductory note to this story is therefore entirely appropriate. *Paupers' Graves* is a story I told myself when I shut my eyes. In the dark. Where the dead tell their own stories and where they can hear mine…

Unlike the characters in the story, I hope I've not been damned as a result.

Bio:

James Everington mainly writes dark, supernatural fiction, although he occasionally takes a break and writes dark, non-supernatural fiction. His second collection of such tales, *Falling Over*, is out now from Infinity Plus.

2016 saw the release of a ghostly novella *Trying To Be So Quiet* from Boo Books and *The Quarantined City*, an episodic novel mixing Borgesian strangeness with supernatural horror, from Infinity Plus.

James has had work published in *The Outsiders* (Crystal Lake), *Supernatural Tales*, *Morpheus Tales* and *Little Visible Delight* (Omnium Gatherum), amongst others.

Oh and he drinks Guinness, if anyone's asking. You can find out what James is currently up to at his Scattershot Writing site.

James Everington

Fogbound From 5, Alt-Dead, Alt-Zombie. Siblings, Anatomy of Death, Demons & Devilry and Dead Water. The Curse of the Mummy; Wolf, Ghost, Zombie, Monster & Vampire.
all © Hersham Horror Books 2010-2016

Hersham Horror Books

http://silenthater.wix.com/hersham-horror-books#

Paupers' Graves